FIVE GO OFF IN A CARAVAN

The FAMOUS FIVE *are*
Julian, Dick, George (Georgina by rights),
Anne, and Timothy the dog.

Just when the Five were wondering what
to do for their summer holiday, a circus with
all its gay caravans and performing
animals came along the road. This gave them
the thrilling idea of going off in a caravan
themselves. And thrilling they found it,
for when at last they caught up with the circus
it was plain that some of the characters had
more sinister ways of passing their time than
clowning in the Big Top.

Without Timmy and Pongo the chimpanzee
the criminals would never have got their deserts,
and even Anne, who had wanted an ordinary
holiday, not too exciting, was sorry when
their adventure was all over.

This is the Five's fifth adventure.

Enid Blyton

Five go
off in a caravan

Illustrated by Betty Maxey

KNIGHT BOOKS
Hodder and Stoughton

First published in 1946
This edition first published in 1967
Twenty-fourth impression 1985

Set, printed and bound in Great Britain for Hodder and
Stoughton Paperbacks, a division of Hodder and Stoughton Ltd,
Mill Road, Dunton Green, Sevenoaks, Kent
(Editorial Office: 47 Bedford Square, London WC1 3DP)
by Cox & Wyman Ltd, Reading

ISBN 0 340 04001 7

CONTENTS

Chapter One

THE BEGINNING OF THE HOLIDAYS

'I DO love the beginning of the summer hols,' said Julian. 'They always seem to stretch out ahead for ages and ages.'

'They go so nice and slowly at first,' said Anne, his little sister. 'Then they start to gallop.'

The others laughed. They knew exactly what Anne meant. 'Woof,' said a deep voice, as if someone else thoroughly agreed too.

'Timmy thinks you're right, Anne,' said George, and patted the big dog lying panting beside them. Dick patted him, too, and Timmy licked them both.

The four children were lying in a sunny garden in the first week of the holidays. Usually they went to their cousin Georgina's home for holidays, at Kirrin – but this time, for a change, they were all at the home of Julian, Dick and Anne.

Julian was the oldest, a tall, sturdy boy with a strong and pleasant face. Dick and Georgina came next. Georgina looked more like a curly-headed boy than a girl, and she insisted on being called George. Even the teachers at school called her George. Anne was the youngest, though, much to her delight, she was really growing taller now.

'Daddy said this morning that if we didn't want to stay here all the hols we could choose what we wanted to do,' said Anne. 'I vote for staying here.'

'We could go off somewhere just for two weeks, per-haps,' said Dick. 'For a change.'

'Shall we go to Kirrin, and stay with George's mother and father for a bit?' said Julian, thinking that perhaps George would like this.

'No,' said George at once. 'I went home at half-term, and Mother said Father was just beginning one of his experiments in something or other – and you know what *that* means. If we go there we'd have to walk about on tiptoe, and talk in whispers, and keep out of his way the whole time.'

'That's the worst of having a scientist for a father,' said Dick, lying down on his back and shutting his eyes. 'Well, your mother couldn't cope with us and with your father, too, in the middle of one of his experiments at the same time. Sparks would fly.'

'I like Uncle Quentin, but I'm afraid of him when he's in one of his tempers,' said Anne. 'He shouts so.'

'It's decided that we won't go to Kirrin, then,' said Julian, yawning. 'Not these hols, anyhow. You can always go and see Mother for a week or so, George, when you want to. What shall we do, then? Stay here all the time?'

They were now all lying down on their backs in the sun, their eyes shut. What a hot afternoon! Timmy sat up by George, his pink tongue hanging out, panting loudly.

'Don't, Timmy,' said Anne. 'You sound as if you have been running for miles, and you make me feel hotter than ever.'

Timmy put a friendly paw on Anne's middle and she squealed. 'Oh, Timmy – your paw's heavy. Take it off.'

'You know, I think if we were allowed to go off by our-selves somewhere, it would be rather fun,' said George, biting a blade of grass and squinting up into the deep blue sky. 'The biggest fun we've ever had was when we were alone on Kirrin Island, for instance. Couldn't we go off somewhere all by ourselves?'

'But where?' said Dick. 'And how? I mean we aren't old enough to take a car – though I bet I could drive one. It wouldn't be much fun going on bicycles, because Anne can't ride as fast as we can.'

'And somebody always gets a puncture,' said Julian.

'It would be jolly good fun to go off on horses,' said George. 'Only we haven't got even one.'

'Yes, we have – there's old Dobby down in the field,' said Dick. 'He is ours. He used to draw the pony-cart, but we don't use it any more now he's turned out to grass.'

'Well, one horse wouldn't take four of us, silly,' said George. 'Dobby's no good.'

There was a silence, and everyone thought lazily about holidays. Timmy snapped at a fly, and his teeth came together with a loud click.

'Wish I could catch flies like that,' said Dick, flapping away a blue-bottle. 'Come and catch this one, Timmy, old thing.'

'What about a walking tour?' said Julian after a pause. There was a chorus of groans.

'What! In this weather! You're mad!'

'We shouldn't be allowed to.'

'All right, all right,' said Julian. 'Think of a better idea, then.'

'I'd like to go somewhere where we could bathe,' said

Anne. 'In a lake, for instance, if we can't go to the sea.'

'Sounds nice,' said Dick. 'My goodness, I'm sleepy. Let's hurry up and settle this matter, or I shall be snoring hard.'

But it wasn't easy to settle. Nobody wanted to go off to an hotel, or to rooms. Grown-ups would want to go with them and look after them. And nobody wanted to go walking or cycling in the hot August weather.

'Looks as if we'll have to stay at home all the hols, then,' said Julian. 'Well – I'm going to have a snooze.'

In two minutes they were all asleep on the grass except Timmy. If his family fell asleep like this, Timmy considered himself on guard. The big dog gave his mistress George a soft lick and sat up firmly beside her, his ears cocked, and his eyes bright. He panted hard, but nobody heard him. They were all snoozing deliciously in the sun, getting browner and browner.

The garden sloped up a hillside. From where he sat Timmy could see quite a long way, both up and down the road that ran by the house. It was a wide road, but not a very busy one, for it was a country district.

Timmy heard a dog barking in the distance, and his ears twitched in that direction. He heard people walking down the road and his ears twitched again. He missed nothing, not even the robin that flew down to get a caterpillar on a bush not far off. He growled softly in his throat at the robin – just to tell it that he was on guard, so beware.

Then something came down the wide road, something that made Timmy shake with excitement, and sniff at the strange smells that came floating up to the garden. A big procession came winding up the road, with a rumble and clatter of wheels – a slow procession, headed by a very strange thing.

Timmy had no idea what it was that headed the procession. Actually it was a big elephant, and Timmy smelt its smell, strange and strong, and didn't like it. He smelt the scent of the monkeys in their travelling cage, too, and he heard the barking of the performing dogs in their van.

He answered them defiantly. 'WOOF, WOOF, WOOF.'

The loud barking awoke all four children at once. 'Shut up, Timmy,' said George crossly. 'What a row to make when we're all having a nap.'

'WOOF,' said Timmy obstinately, and pawed at his mistress to make her sit up and take notice. George sat up. She saw the procession at once and gave a yell.

'Hey, you others. There's a circus procession going by. Look.'

They all sat up, wide awake now. They stared down at the caravans going slowly along, and listened to an animal howling, and the dogs barking.

'Look at that elephant, pulling the caravan along,' said Anne. 'He must be jolly strong.'

'Let's go down to the gate of the drive and watch,' said Dick. So they all got up and ran down the garden, then round the house and into the drive that led to the road. The procession was just passing the gates.

It was a gay sight. The caravans were painted in brilliant colours, and looked spick and span from the outside. Little flowery curtains hung at the windows. At the front of each caravan sat the man or woman who owned it, driving the horse that pulled it. Only the front caravan was pulled by an elephant.

'Golly – doesn't it look exciting?' said George. 'I wish I belonged to a circus that went wandering all over the place all the year. That's just the sort of life I'd like.'

'Fat lot of good you'd be in the circus,' said Dick rudely. 'You can't even turn a cart-wheel.'

'What's a cart-wheel?' said Anne.

'What that boy's doing over there,' said Dick. 'Look.'

He pointed to a boy who was turning cart-wheels very quickly, going over and over on his hands and feet, turning himself like a wheel. It looked so easy, but it wasn't, as Dick very well knew.

'Oh, is he turning a cart-wheel?' said Anne admiringly. 'I wish I could do that.'

The boy came up to them and grinned. He had two

terrier dogs with him. Timmy growled and George put
her hand on his collar.

'Don't come too near,' she called. 'Timmy isn't quite
sure about you.'

'We won't hurt him!' said the boy, and grinned again.
He had an ugly, freckled face, with a shock of untidy
hair. 'I won't let my dogs eat your Timmy.'

'As if they could!' began George scornfully, and then
laughed. The terriers kept close to the boy's heels. He
clicked and both dogs rose at once on their hind legs and
walked sedately behind him with funny little steps.

'Oh – are they performing dogs?' said Anne. 'Are they
yours?'

'These two are,' said, the boy. This is Barker and this

is Growler. I've had them from pups – clever as paint they are!'

'Woof,' said Timmy, apparently disgusted at seeing dogs walk in such a peculiar way. It had never occurred to him that a dog could get up on his hind legs.

'Where are you giving your next show?' asked George eagerly. 'We'd like to see it.'

'We're off for a rest,' said the boy. 'Up in the hills, where there's a blue lake at the bottom. We're allowed to camp there with our animals – it's wild and lonely and we don't disturb nobody. We just camp there with our caravans.'

'It sounds fine,' said Dick. 'Which is your caravan?'

'This one, just coming' said the boy, and he pointed to a brightly painted van, whose sides were blue and yellow, and whose wheels were red. 'I live in it with my Uncle Dan. He's the chief clown of the circus. There he is, sitting on the front, driving the horse.'

The children stared at the chief clown, and thought that they had never seen anyone less like a clown. He was dressed in dirty grey flannel trousers and a dirty red shirt open at an equally dirty neck.

He didn't look as if he could make a single joke, or do anything in the least funny. In fact, he looked really bad-tempered, the children thought, and he scowled so fiercely as he chewed on an old pipe that Anne felt quite scared. He didn't look at the children at all, but called in a sharp voice to the boy:

'Nobby! You come on along of us. Get in the caravan and make me a cup of tea.'

The boy Nobby winked at the children and ran to the caravan. It was plain that Uncle Dan kept him in order all right! He poked his head out of the little window in the side of the caravan nearest to the children.

'Sorry I can't ask you to tea too!' he called. 'And the dog. Barker and Growler wouldn't half like to know him!'

The caravan passed on, taking the scowling clown with it, and the grinning Nobby. The children watched the others going by, too; it was quite a big circus. There was a cage of monkeys, a chimpanzee sitting in a corner of a dark cage, asleep, a string of beautiful horses, sleek and shining, a great wagon carrying benches and forms and tents, caravans for the circus folk to live in, and a host of interesting people to see, sitting on the steps of their vans or walking together outside to stretch their legs.

At last the procession was gone and the children went slowly back to their sunny corner in the garden. They sat down – and then George announced something that made them sit up straight.

'*I* know what we'll do these hols! We'll hire a caravan and go off in it by ourselves. Do let's! Oh, do let's!'

Chapter Two

GEORGE'S GREAT IDEA

THE others stared at George's excited face. She had gone quite red. Dick thumped on the ground.

'A jolly good idea! Why didn't we think of it before?'

'Oh, *yes*! A caravan to ourselves! It sounds too good to be true!' said Anne, and her eyes shone.

'Well, I must say it would be something we've never done before,' said Julian, wondering if it was really possible. 'I say – wouldn't it be gorgeous if we could go off into the hills – where that lake is that the boy spoke about? We could bathe there – and we could perhaps get to know the circus folk. I've always wanted to know about circuses.'

'Oh, *Julian*! That's a better idea still!' said George, rubbing her hands together in delight. 'I liked that boy Nobby, didn't you?'

'Yes,' said everyone.

'But I didn't like his uncle,' said Dick. 'He looked a nasty bit of work. I bet he makes Nobby toe the mark and do what he's told.'

'Julian, do you think we'd be allowed to go caravanning by ourselves?' asked Anne earnestly. 'It does seem to me to be the most marvellous idea we've ever had.'

'Well – we can ask and see,' said Julian. 'I'm old enough to look after you all.'

'Pooh!' said George. 'I don't want any looking after, thank you. And anyway, if we want looking after, Timmy

can do that. I bet the grown-ups will be glad to be rid of
us for a week or two. They always think the summer hols
are too long.'

'We'll take Dobby with us to pull the caravan!' said
Anne suddenly, looking down at the field where Dobby
stood, patiently flicking away the flies with his long tail.
'Dobby would love that! I always think he must be lonely,
living in that field all by himself, just being borrowed by
people occasionally.'

'Of course – Dobby could come,' said Dick. 'That
would be fine. Where could we get the caravan from?
Are they easy to hire?'

'Don't know,' said Julian. 'I knew a chap at school –
you remember him, Dick, that big fellow called Perry –
he used to go caravanning every hols with his people.
They used to hire caravans, I know. I might find out
from him where he got them from.'

'Daddy will know,' said Anne. 'Or Mummy. Grown-
ups always know things like that. I'd like a nice large
caravan – red and blue – with a little chimney, and
windows each side, and a door at the back, and steps to
go up into the caravan, and . . .'

The others interrupted with their own ideas, and soon
they were all talking excitedly about it – so loudly that
they didn't see someone walking up and standing near by,
laughing at the excitement.

'Woof,' said Timmy politely. He was the only one who
had ears and eyes for anything else at the moment. The
children looked up.

'Oh, hallo, Mother!' said Julian. 'You've just come at
the right moment. We want to tell you about an idea
we've got.'

His mother sat down, smiling. 'You seem very excited about something,' she said. 'What is it?'

'Well, it's like this, Mummy,' said Anne, before anyone else could get a word in, 'we've made up our minds that we'd like to go off in a caravan for a holiday by ourselves! Oh, Mummy – it would be such fun!'

'By yourselves?' said her mother doubtfully. 'Well, I don't know about that.'

'Julian can look after us,' said Anne.

'So can Timmy,' put in George at once, and Timmy thumped the ground with his tail. Of course he could look after them! Hadn't he done it for years, and shared all their adventures? Thump, thump, thump!

'I'll have to talk it over with Daddy,' said Mother. 'Now don't look so disappointed – I can't decide a thing like this all by myself in a hurry. But it may fit in quite well because I know Daddy has to go up north for a little while, and he would like me to go with him. So he might think a little caravanning quite a good idea. I'll talk to him tonight.'

'We could have Dobby to pull the caravan, Mummy,' said Anne, her eyes bright. 'Couldn't we? He'd love to come. He has such a dull life now.'

'We'll see, we'll see,' said her mother, getting up. 'Now you'd better all come in and wash. It's nearly tea-time. Your hair is terrible, Anne. What *have* you been doing?'

Everyone rushed indoors to wash, feeling distinctly cheerful. Mother hadn't said NO. She had even thought it might fit in quite well. Golly, to go off in a caravan all alone – doing their own cooking and washing – having Dobby for company, and Timmy as well, of course. How simply gorgeous.

The children's father did not come home until late that evening, which was a nuisance, for nobody felt that they could wait for very long to know whether they might or might not go. Everyone but Julian was in bed when he came home, and even when he, too, came to bed he had nothing to report.

He stuck his head into the girls' bedroom. 'Daddy's tired and he's having a late supper, and Mother won't bother him till he's feeling better. So we shan't know till morning, worse luck!'

The girls groaned. How could they possibly go to sleep with thoughts of caravans floating deliciously in their heads – not knowing whether or not they would be allowed to go!

'Blow!' said George. 'I shan't go to sleep for ages. Get off my feet, Timmy. Honestly, it's too hot to have you anywhere near me this weather.'

In the morning good news awaited the four children. They sat down at the breakfast-table, all very punctual for once, and Julian looked expectantly at his mother. She smiled at him and nodded.

'Yes, we've talked it over,' she said. 'And Daddy says he doesn't see why you shouldn't have a caravan holiday. He thinks it would be good for you to go off and rough it a bit. But you will have to have two caravans, not one. We couldn't have all four of you, and Timmy too, living in one caravan.'

'Oh – but Dobby couldn't pull *two* caravans, Mummy,' said Anne.

'We can borrow another horse,' said Julian. 'Can't we, Mother? Thanks awfully, Daddy, for saying we can go. It's jolly sporting of you.'

'Absolutely super,' said Dick.

'Wizard!' said George, her fingers scratching Timmy's head excitedly. 'When can we go? Tomorrow?'

'Of course not!' said Julian. 'We've got to get the caravans – and borrow a horse – and pack – and all sorts of things.'

'You can go next week, when I take your mother up north with me,' said his father. 'That will suit us very well. We can give Cook a holiday, too, then. You will have to send us a card every single day to tell us how you are and where you are.'

'It does sound thrilling,' said Anne. 'I really don't feel as if I can eat any breakfast, Mummy.'

'Well, if that's the effect the idea of caravanning has on you, I don't think you'd better go,' said her mother. Anne hastily began to eat her shredded wheat, and her appetite soon came back. It was too good to be true – to have *two* caravans – and *two* horses – and sleep in bunks perhaps – and cook meals outside in the open air – and . . .

'You will be in complete charge, you understand, Julian,' said the boy's father. 'You are old enough now to be really responsible. The others must realise that you are in charge and they must do as you say.'

'Yes, sir,' said Julian, feeling proud. 'I'll see to things all right.'

'And Timmy will be in charge, too,' said George. 'He's just as responsible as Julian.'

'Woof,' said Timmy, hearing his name, and thumping the floor with his tail.

'You're a darling, Timmy,' said Anne. 'I'll always do what *you* say, as well as what Julian says!'

'Idiot!' said Dick. He patted Timmy's head. 'I bet we wouldn't be allowed to go without you, Timothy. You are a jolly good guard for anyone.'

'You certainly wouldn't be allowed to go without Timmy,' said his mother. 'We know you'll be safe with him.'

It was all most exciting. The children went off to talk things over by themselves when breakfast was finished.

'I vote we go caravanning up into the hills that boy spoke of, where the lake lies at the bottom – and camp there,' said Julian. 'We'd have company then – jolly exciting company, too. We wouldn't live *too* near the circus camp – they might not like strangers butting in – but we'll live near enough to see the elephant going for his daily walk, and the dogs being exercised . . .'

'And we'll make friends with Nobby, won't we?' said Anne eagerly. 'I liked him. We won't go near his uncle, though. I think it's queer that such a bad-tempered looking man should be the chief clown in a circus.'

'I wonder when and where Mother will get the caravans!' said Julian. 'Gosh, won't it be fun when we see them for the first time!'

'Let's go and tell Dobby!' said Anne. 'He is sure to be excited, too!'

'Baby! He won't understand a word you tell him!' said George. But off she went with Anne just the same, and soon Dobby was hearing all about the wonderful holiday plan. Hrrrrumph! So long as it included him, too, he was happy!

Chapter Three

THE CARAVANS ARRIVE

At last the great day came when the two caravans were due to arrive. The children stood at the end of the drive for hours, watching for them.

Mother had managed to borrow them from an old friend of hers. The children had promised faithfully to look after them well, and not to damage anything. Now they stood at the end of the drive, watching eagerly for the caravans to arrive.

'They are being drawn by cars today,' said Julian. 'But they are fitted up to be horse-drawn, too. I wonder what they are like – and what colour they are?'

'Will they be like gypsy caravans, on high wheels, do you think?' asked Anne. Julian shook his head.

'No, they're modern, Mother says. Streamlined and all that. Not too big either, because a horse can't draw too heavy a van.'

'They're coming, they're coming! I can see them!' suddenly yelled George, making them all jump. 'Look, isn't that them, far down the road?'

They all looked hard into the distance. No one had such good eyes as George, and all they could see was a blotch, a moving speck far away on the road. But George's eyes saw two caravans, one behind the other.

'George is right,' said Julian, straining his eyes. 'It's our caravans. They're each drawn by a small car.'

'One's red and the other's green,' said Anne. 'Bags I the red one. Oh, hurry up, caravans!'

At last they were near enough to see properly. The children ran to meet them. They certainly were very nice ones, quite modern and 'streamlined', as Julian had said, well built and comfortable.

'They almost reach the ground!' said Anne. 'And look at the wheels, set so neatly into the side of the vans. I do like the red one, bags I the red one.'

Each van had a little chimney, long, narrow windows down the two sides, and tiny ones in front by the driver's seat. There was a broad door at the back and two steps down. Pretty curtains fluttered at the open windows.

'Red curtains for the green caravan, and green ones for the red caravan!' said Anne. 'Oh, I want to go inside!'

But she couldn't because the doors were locked. So she had to be content to run with the others up the drive after the two caravans, shouting loudly:

'Mummy! They're here, the caravans are here.'

Her mother came running down the steps to see. Soon the doors were unlocked and the children went inside the caravans. Delighted shouts came from both vans.

'Bunks along one side – is that where we sleep? How gorgeous!'

'Look at this little sink – we can really wash up. And golly, water comes out of these taps!'

'There's a proper stove to cook on – but I vote we cook out of doors on a camp fire. I say, look at the bright frying-pans – and all the cups and saucers hanging up!'

'It's like a proper little house inside. Doesn't it seem nice and *big*? Mother, isn't it beautifully planned? Don't you wish you were coming with us?'

'Hey, you girls! Do you see where the water comes from? Out of that tank on the roof. It must collect rainwater. And look at this gadget for heating water. Isn't it all super?'

The children spent hours examining their caravans and finding out all the secrets. They certainly were very well fitted, spotlessly clean, and very roomy. George felt as if she couldn't wait to start out. She really must get Dobby and set out at once!

'No, you must wait, silly,' said Julian. 'You know we've to get the other horse. He's not coming till tomorrow.'

The other horse was a sturdy little black fellow called Trotter. He belonged to the milkman, who often lent him out. He was a sensible little horse, and the children knew him very well and liked him. They all learnt riding at school, and knew how to groom and look after a horse, so there would be no difficulty over their managing Dobby and Trotter.

Mother was thrilled over the caravans, too, and looked very longingly at them. 'If I wasn't going with Daddy I should be most tempted to come with you,' she said. 'Don't look so startled, Anne dear – I'm not really coming!'

'We're jolly lucky to get such decent caravans,' said Julian. 'We'd better pack our things today, hadn't we, Mother – and start off tomorrow, now we've got the caravans.'

'You won't need to pack,' said his mother. 'All you have to do is to pop your things straight into the cupboards and drawers – you will only want clothes and books and a few games to play in case it's rainy.'

'We don't need any clothes except our night things, do

we?' said George, who would have lived in a jersey and jeans all day and every day if she had been allowed to.

'You must take plenty of jerseys, another pair of jeans each, in case you get wet, your rain-coats, bathing-things, towels, a change of shoes, night things, and some cool shirts or blouses,' said Mother. Everyone groaned.

'What a frightful lot of things!' said Dick. 'There'll never be room for all those.'

'Oh yes there will,' said Mother. 'You will be sorry if you take too few clothes, get soaked through, have nothing to change into, and catch fearful colds that will stop you from enjoying a lovely holiday like this.'

'Come on, let's get the things,' said Dick. 'Once Mother starts off about catching cold there's no knowing what else she'll make us take – is there, Mother?'

'You're a cheeky boy,' said his mother, smiling. 'Yes, go and collect your things. I'll help you to put them into the cupboards and drawers. Isn't it marvellous how everything folds so neatly into the walls of the caravans – there seems to be room for everything, and you don't notice the cupboards.'

'I shall keep everything very clean,' said Anne. 'You know how I like *playing* at keeping house, don't you, Mother – well, it will be real this time. I shall have two caravans to keep clean, all by myself.'

'All by yourself!' said her mother. 'Well, surely the boys will help you – and certainly George must.'

'Pooh, the boys!' said Anne. 'They won't know how to wash and dry a cup properly – and George never bothers about things like that. If I don't make the bunks and wash the crockery, they would never be made or washed, I know that!'

'Well, it's a good thing that one of you is sensible!' said her mother. 'You'll find that everyone will share in the work, Anne. Now off you go and get your things. Bring all the rain-coats, to start with.'

It was fun taking things down to the caravans and packing them all in. There were shelves for a few books and games, so Julian brought down snap cards, ludo, lexicon, happy families and dominoes, as well as four or five books for each of them. He also brought down some maps of the district, because he meant to plan out where they were to go, and the best roads to follow.

Daddy had given him a useful little book in which were the names of farms that would give permission to caravanners to camp in fields for the night. 'You must always choose a field where there is a stream, if possible,' said his father, 'because Dobby and Trotter will want water.'

'Remember to boil every drop of water you drink,' said the children's mother. 'That's very important. Get as much milk from the farms as they will let you have. And remember that there is plenty of ginger-beer in the locker under the second caravan.'

'It's all so thrilling,' said Anne, peering down to look at the locker into which Julian had put the bottles of ginger-beer. 'I can't believe we're really going tomorrow.'

But it was true. Dobby and Trotter were to be taken to the caravans the next day and harnessed. How exciting for them, too, Anne thought.

Timmy couldn't quite understand all the excitement, but he shared in it, of course, and kept his tail on the wag all day long. He examined the caravans thoroughly from end to end, found a rug he liked the smell of, and lay down on it. 'This is *my* corner,' he seemed to say. 'If you go off in these peculiar houses on wheels, this is my own little corner.'

'We'll have the red caravan, George,' said Anne. 'The boys can have the green one. They don't care what colour they have – but I love red. I say, won't it be sport to sleep in those bunks? They look jolly comfortable.'

At last tomorrow came – and the milkman brought the sturdy little black horse, Trotter, up the drive. Julian fetched Dobby from the field. The horses nuzzled one another and Dobby said 'Hrrrumph' in a very civil horsey voice.

'They're going to like each other,' said Anne. 'Look at them nuzzling. Trotter, you're going to draw *my* caravan.'

The two horses stood patiently while they were harnessed. Dobby jerked his head once or twice as if he was impatient to be off and stamped a little.

'Oh, Dobby, I feel like that, too!' said Anne. 'Don't you, Dick, don't you, Julian?'

'I do rather,' said Dick with a grin. 'Get up there, Dobby – that's right. Who's going to drive, Julian – take it in turns, shall we?'

'I'm going to drive *our* caravan,' said George. 'Anne wouldn't be any good at it, though I'll let her have a turn at it sometimes. Driving is a man's job.'

'Well, you're only a girl!' said Anne indignantly. 'You're not a man, nor even a boy!'

George put on one of her scowls. She always wanted to be a boy, and even thought of herself as one. She didn't like to be reminded that she was only a girl. But not even George could scowl for long that exciting morning! She

soon began to caper round and about again, laughing
and calling out with the others:

'We're ready! Surely we're ready!'

'Yes. Do let's go! JULIAN! He's gone indoors, the idiot,
just when we want to start.'

'He's gone to get the cakes that Cook has baked this
morning for us. We've heaps of food in the larder. I feel
hungry already.'

'Here's Julian. Do come on, Julian. We'll drive off
without you. Good-bye, Mother! We'll send you a card
every single day, we faithfully promise.'

Julian got up on the front of the green caravan. He
clicked to Dobby. 'Get on, Dobby! We're off! Good-bye,
Mother!'

Dick sat beside him, grinning with pure happiness. The
caravans moved off down the drive. George pulled at
Trotter's reins and the little horse followed the caravan
in front. Anne, sitting beside George, waved wildly.

'Good-bye, Mother! We're off at last on another
adventure. Hurrah! Three cheers! Hurrah!'

Chapter Four

AWAY THEY GO!

THE caravans went slowly down the wide road. Julian was so happy that he sang at the top of his voice, and the others joined in the choruses. Timmy barked excitedly. He was sitting on one side of George and as Anne was on the other George was decidedly squashed. But little things like that did not bother her at all.

Dobby plodded on slowly, enjoying the sunshine and the little breeze that raised the hairs on his mane. Trotter followed at a short distance. He was very much interested in Timmy, and always turned his head when the dog barked or got down for a run. It was fun to have two horses and a dog to travel with.

It had been decided that they should make their way towards the hills where they hoped to find the circus. Julian had traced the place in his map. He was sure it must be right because of the lake that lay in the valley at the foot of the hills.

'See?' he said to the others, pointing. 'There it is – Lake Merran. I bet we'll find the circus camp somewhere near it. It would be a very good place for all their animals – no one to interfere with the camp, plenty of water for both animals and men, and probably good farms to supply them with food.'

'We'll have to find a good farm ourselves tonight,' said Dick. 'And ask permission to camp. Lucky we've got that little book telling us where to go and ask.'

Anne thought with delight of the coming evening, when they would stop and camp, cook a meal, drowse over a camp fire, and go to sleep in the little bunks. She didn't know which was nicer – ambling along down country lanes with the caravans – or preparing to settle in for the night. She was sure it was going to be the nicest holiday they had ever had.

'Don't you think so?' she asked George as they sat together on the driving-seat, with Timmy, for once, trotting beside the caravan, and leaving them a little more room than usual. 'You know, most of our hols have been packed with adventures – awfully exciting, I know – but I'd like an *ordinary* holiday now, wouldn't you – not *too* exciting.'

'Oh, I like adventures,' said George, shaking the reins and making Trotter do a little trot. 'I wouldn't a bit mind having another one. But we shan't this time, Anne. No such luck!'

They stopped for a meal at half-past twelve, all of them feeling very hungry. Dobby and Trotter moved towards a ditch in which long, juicy grass grew, and munched away happily.

The children lay on a sunny bank and ate and drank. Anne looked at George. 'You've got more freckles these hols, George, than you ever had in your life before.'

'That doesn't worry *me*!' said George, who never cared in the least how she looked, and was even angry with her hair for being too curly, and making her look too much like a girl. 'Pass the sandwiches, Anne – the tomato ones – golly, if we always feel as hungry as this we'll have to buy eggs and bacon and butter and milk at every farm we pass!'

They set off again. Dick took his turn at driving Dobby, and Julian walked to stretch his legs. George still wanted to drive, but Anne felt too sleepy to sit beside her with safety.

'If I shut my eyes and sleep I shall fall off the seat,' she said. 'I'd better go into the caravan and sleep there.'

So in she went, all by herself. It was cool and dim inside the caravan, for the curtains had been pulled across the window to keep the inside cool. Anne climbed on to one of the bunks and lay down. She shut her eyes. The caravan rumbled slowly on, and the little girl fell asleep.

Julian peeped in at her and grinned. Timmy came and looked, too, but Julian wouldn't let him go in and wake Anne by licking her.

'You come and walk with me, Tim,' he said. 'You're getting fat. Exercise will do you good.'

'He's *not* getting fat!' called George, indignantly. 'He's a very nice shape. Don't you listen to him, Timothy.'

'Woof,' said Timmy, and trotted along at Julian's heels.

The two caravans covered quite a good distance that day, even though they went slowly. Julian did not miss the way once. He was very good indeed at map-reading. Anne was disappointed that they could not see the hills they were making for, at the end of the day.

'Goodness, they're miles and miles away!' said Julian. 'We shan't arrive for at least four or five days, silly! Now, look out for a farm, kids. There should be one near here, where we can ask permission to camp for the night.'

'There's one, surely,' said George, after a few minutes. She pointed to where a red-roofed building with moss-covered barns, stood glowing in the evening sun. Hens clucked about it, and a dog or two watched them from a gateway.

'Yes, that's the one,' said Julian, examining his map. 'Longman's Farm. There should be a stream near it. There it is, look – in that field. Now, if we could get permission to camp just here, it would be lovely.'

Julian went to the farm to see the farmer, and Anne went with him to ask for eggs. The farmer was not there, but the farmer's wife, who liked the look of the tall, well-spoken Julian very much, gave them permission at once to spend the night in the field by the stream.

'I know you won't leave a lot of litter, or go chasing the farm animals,' she said. 'Or leave the gates open like some ill-bred campers do. And what's that you want, Missy – some new-laid eggs. Yes, of course, you can have some – and you can pick the ripe plums off that tree, too, to go with your supper!'

There was bacon in the larder of the caravans, and Anne said she would fry that and an egg each for everyone. She was very proud of being able to cook them. She had taken a few lessons from Cook in the last few days, and was very anxious to show the others what she had learnt.

Julian said it was too hot to cook in the caravan, and he built her a fine fire in the field. Dick set the two horses free and they wandered off to the stream, where they stood knee-high in the cool water, enjoying it immensely. Trotter muzzled against Dobby, and then tried to nuzzle down to Timmy, too, when the big dog came to drink beside him.

'Doesn't the bacon smell lovely?' called Anne to George,

who was busy getting plates and mugs out of the red
caravan. 'Let's have ginger-beer to drink, George. I'm
jolly thirsty. Watch me crack these eggs on the edge of
this cup, everybody, so that I can get out the yolk and
white and fry them.'

Crack! The egg broke against the edge of the cup – but
its contents unfortunately fell outside the cup instead of
inside. Anne went red when everyone roared with
laughter.

Timmy came and licked up the mess. He was very
useful for that sort of thing. 'You'd make a good dust-bin,
Timmy,' said Anne. 'Here's a bit of bacon-rind, too.
Catch!'

Anne fried the bacon and eggs really well. The others
were most admiring, even George, and they all cleared
their plates well, wiping the last bit of fat off with bread,
so that they would be easy to wash.

'Do you think Timmy would like me to fry him a few
dog-biscuits, instead of having them cold?' said Anne,
suddenly. 'Fried things are so nice. I'm sure Timmy
would like fried biscuits better than ordinary ones.'

'Well, he wouldn't,' said George. 'They would just
make him sick.'

'How do you know?' said Anne. 'You can't possibly
tell.'

'I always know what Timmy would really like and
what he wouldn't,' said George. 'And he wouldn't like
his biscuits fried. Pass the plums, Dick. They look super.'

They lingered over the little camp-fire for a long time,
and then Julian said it was time for bed. Nobody
minded, because they all wanted to try sleeping on the
comfortable-looking bunks.

'Shall I wash at the stream or in the little sink where I washed the plates?' said Anne. 'I don't know which would be nicer.'

'There's more water to spare in the stream,' said Julian. 'Hurry up, won't you, because I want to lock your caravan door so that you'll be safe.'

'Lock our door!' said George, indignantly. 'You jolly well won't! Nobody's going to lock *me* in! I might think I'd like to take a walk in the moonlight or something.'

'Yes, but a tramp or somebody might . . .' began Julian. George interrupted him scornfully.

'What about Timmy? You know jolly well he'd never let anyone come *near* our caravans, let alone into them! I won't be locked in, Julian. I couldn't bear it. Timmy's better than any locked door.'

'Well, I suppose he is,' said Julian. 'All right, don't look so furious, George. Walk half the night in moonlight if you want to – though there won't be any moon tonight, I'm sure. Golly, I'm sleepy!'

They climbed into the two caravans, after washing in the stream. They all undressed, and got into the inviting bunks. There was a sheet, one blanket and a rug – but all the children threw off both blanket and rug and kept only a sheet over them that hot night.

At first Anne tried sleeping in the lower bunk, beneath George – but Timmy would keep on trying to clamber up to get to George. He wanted to lie on her feet as usual. Anne got cross.

'George! You'd better change places with me. Timmy keeps jumping on me and walking all over me trying to get up to your bunk. I'll never get to sleep.'

So George changed places, and after that Timmy made no more noise, but lay contentedly at the end of George's bunk on the rolled-up blanket, while Anne lay in the bunk above, trying not to go to sleep because it was such a lovely feeling to be inside a caravan that stood by a stream in a field.

Owls hooted to one another, and Timmy growled softly. The voice of the stream, contented and babbling, could be quite clearly heard now that everything was so quiet. Anne felt her eyes closing. Oh dear – she would simply *have* to go to sleep.

But something suddenly awoke her with a jump, and Timmy barked so loudly that both Anne and George almost fell out of their bunks in fright. Something bumped violently against the caravan, and shook it from end to end! Was somebody trying to get in?

Timmy leapt to the floor and ran to the door, which George had left open a little because of the heat. Then the voices of Dick and Julian were heard.

'What's up? Are you girls all right? We're coming!' And over the wet grass raced the two boys in their dressing-gowns. Julian ran straight into something hard and warm and solid. He yelled.

Dick switched on his torch and began to laugh helplessly. 'You ran straight into Dobby. Look at him staring at you! He must have lumbered all round our caravans making the bumps we heard. It's all right, girls. It's only Dobby.'

So back they all went again to sleep, and this time they slept till the morning, not even stirring when Trotter, too, came to nuzzle round the caravan and snort softly in the night.

Chapter Five

THE WAY TO MERRAN LAKE

THE next three or four days were absolutely perfect, the children thought. Blue skies, blazing sun, wayside streams to paddle or bathe in, and two houses on wheels that went rumbling for miles down roads and lanes quite new to them – what could be lovelier for four children all on their own?

Timmy seemed to enjoy everything thoroughly, too, and had made firm friends with Trotter, the little black horse. Trotter was always looking for Timmy to run beside him, and he whinnied to Timmy whenever he wanted him. The two horses were friends, too, and when they were set free at night they made for the stream together, and stood in the water side by side, nuzzling one another happily.

'I like this holiday better than any we've ever had,' said Anne, busily cooking something in a pan. 'It's exciting without being adventurous. And although Julian thinks he's in charge of us, *I* am really! You'd never get your bunks made, or your meals cooked, or the caravans kept clean if it wasn't for me!'

'Don't boast!' said George, feeling rather guilty because she let Anne do so much.

'I'm not boasting!' said Anne, indignantly. 'I'm just telling the truth. Why, you've never even made your own bunk once, George. Not that I mind doing it. I love having two houses on wheels to look after.'

'You're a very good little housekeeper,' said Julian. 'We couldn't possibly do without you!'

Anne blushed with pride. She took the pan off the camp-fire and put the contents on to four plates. 'Come along!' she called, in a voice just like her mother's. 'Have your meal while it's hot.'

'I'd rather have mine when it's cold, thank you,' said George. 'It doesn't seem to have got a bit cooler, even though it's evening-time.'

They had been on the road four days now, and Anne had given up looking for the hills where they hoped to find the circus folk camping. In fact she secretly hoped they wouldn't find them, because she was so much enjoying the daily wanderings over the lovely countryside.

Timmy came to lick the plates. The children always let him do that now because it made them so much easier to wash. Anne and George took the things down to a little brown brook to rinse, and Julian took out his map.

He and Dick pored over it. 'We're just about here,' said Julian, pointing. 'And if so, it looks as if tomorrow we ought to come to those hills above the lake. Then we should see the circus.'

'Good!' said Dick. 'I hope Nobby will be there. He would love to show us round, I'm sure. He would show us a good place to camp, too, perhaps.'

'Oh, we can find that ourselves,' said Julian, who now rather prided himself on picking excellent camping-sites. 'Anyway, I don't want to be *too* near the circus. It might be a bit smelly. I'd rather be up in the hills some way above it. We'll get a place with a lovely view.'

'Right,' said Dick, and Julian folded up the map. The two girls came back with the clean crockery, and Anne put it neatly back on the shelves in the red caravan. Trotter came to look for Timmy, who was lying panting under George's caravan.

Timmy wouldn't budge, so Trotter tried to get under the caravan too. But he couldn't possibly, of course, for he was much too big. So he lay down on the shady side, as near to Timmy as he could get.

'Trotter's really a comic horse,' said Dick. 'He'd be quite good in a circus, I should think! Did you see him chasing Timmy yesterday – just as if they were playing "He"?'

The word 'circus' reminded them of Nobby and his circus, and they began to talk eagerly of all the animals there.

'I liked the look of the elephant,' said George. 'I wonder what his name is. And wouldn't I like to hold a monkey!'

'I bet that chimpanzee's clever,' said Dick. 'I wonder what Timmy will think of him. I hope he'll get on all right with all the animals, especially the other dogs.'

'I hope we don't see much of Nobby's uncle,' said Anne. 'He looked as if he'd like to box anybody's ears if they so much as answered him back.'

'Well, he won't box *mine*,' said Julian. 'We'll keep out of his way. He doesn't look a very pleasant chap, I must say. Perhaps he won't be there.'

'Timmy, come out from under the caravan!' called George. 'It's quite cool and shady where we are. Come on!'

He came, panting. Trotter immediately got up and came with him. The little horse lay down beside Timmy and nuzzled him. Timmy gave his nose a lick and then turned away, looking bored.

'Isn't Trotter funny?' said Anne. 'Timmy, what *will* you think of all the circus animals, I wonder! I do hope we see the circus tomorrow. Shall we get as far as the hills, Julian? Though really I shan't mind a bit if we don't; it's so nice being on our own like this.'

They all looked out for the hills the next day as the caravans rumbled slowly down the lanes, pulled by Trotter and Dobby. And, in the afternoon, they saw them, blue in the distance.

'There they are!' said Julian. 'Those must be the Merran Hills – and Merran Lake must lie at the foot. I say, I hope the two horses are strong enough to pull the caravans a good way up. There should be an absolutely marvellous view over the lake if we get up high enough.'

The hills came nearer and nearer. They were high ones, and looked lovely in the evening light. Julian looked at his watch.

'We shan't have time to climb them and find a camping site there tonight, I'm afraid,' he said. 'We'd better camp a little way on this evening, and then make our way up into the hills tomorrow morning.'

'All right,' said Dick. 'Anything you say, Captain! There should be a farm about two miles on, according to the book. We'll camp there.'

They came to the farm, which was set by a wide stream that ran swiftly along. Julian went as usual to ask permission to camp, and Dick went with him, leaving the two girls to prepare a meal.

Julian easily got permission, and the farmer's daughter,

a plump jolly girl, sold the boys eggs, bacon, milk, and butter, besides a little crock of yellow cream. She also offered them raspberries from the garden if they liked to pick them and have them with the cream.

'Oh, I say, thanks awfully,' said Julian. 'Could you tell me if there's a circus camping in those hills? Somewhere by the lake.'

'Yes, it went by about a week ago,' said the girl. 'It goes camping there every year, for a rest. I always watch the caravans go by – quite a treat in a quiet place like this! One year they had lions, and at nights I could hear them roaring away. That fair frizzled my spine!'

The boys said good-bye and went off, chuckling to think of the farm-girl's spine being 'fair frizzled' by the roars of the distant lions.

'Well, it looks as if we'll pass the circus camp tomorrow all right,' said Julian. 'I shall enjoy camping up in the hills, won't you, Dick? It will be cooler up there, I expect – usually there's a breeze on the hills.'

'I hope we shan't get our spines fair frizzled by the noise of the circus animals at night,' grinned Dick. 'I feel fair frizzled up by the sun today, I must say!'

The next morning the caravans set off again on what the children hoped would be the last lap of their journey. They would find a lovely camping-place and stay there till they had to go home.

Julian had remembered to send a post-card each day to his parents, telling them where he was, and that everything was fine. He had found out from the farm-girl the right address for that district, and he planned to arrange with the nearest post office to take in any letters for them that came. They had not been able to receive any post, of course, when they were wandering about in their caravans.

Dobby and Trotter walked sedately down the narrow country lane that led towards the hills. Suddenly George caught sight of something flashing blue between the trees.

'Look! There's the lake! Merran Lake!' she shouted. 'Make Dobby go more quickly, Ju. I'm longing to come out into the open and see the lake.'

Soon the lane ended in a broad cart-track that led over a heathery common. The common sloped right down to the edge of an enormous blue lake that lay glittering in the August sunshine.

'I say! Isn't it magnificent?' said Dick, stopping Dobby with a pull. 'Come on, let's get down and go to the edge, Julian. Come on, girls!'

'It's lovely!' said Anne, jumping down from the driving-seat of the red caravan. 'Oh, do let's bathe straight away!'

'Yes, let's,' said Julian, and they all dived into their caravans, stripped off jeans and blouses and pulled on bathing-things. Then, without even a towel to dry themselves on, they tore down to the lake-side, eager to plunge into its blue coolness.

It was very warm at the edge of the water, but further in, where it was deep, the lake was deliciously cold. All the children could swim strongly, and they splashed and yelled in delight. The bottom of the lake was sandy, so the water was as clear as crystal.

When they were tired they all came out and lay on the warm sandy bank of the lake. They dried at once in the sun. Then as soon as they felt too hot in they went again, squealing with joy at the cold water.

'What gorgeous fun to come down here every day and bathe!' said Dick. 'Get away, Timmy, when I'm swimming on my back. Timmy's enjoying the bathe as much as we are, George.'

'Yes, and old Trotter wants to come in, too,' shouted Julian. 'Look at him – he's brought the red caravan right down to the edge of the lake. He'll be in the water with it if we don't stop him!'

They decided to have a picnic by the lake, and to set the horses free to have a bathe if they wanted one. But all they wanted was to drink and to stand knee-high in the water, swishing their tails to keep away the flies that worried them all day long.

'Where's the circus camp?' said George suddenly as they sat munching ham and tomato sandwiches. 'I can't see it.'

The children looked all round the edge of the lake, which stretched as far as they could see. At last George's sharp eyes saw a small spire of smoke rising in the air about a mile or so round the lake.

'The camp must be in that hollow at the foot of the hills over there,' she said. 'I expect the road leads round to it. We'll go that way, shall we, and then go up into the hills behind?'

'Yes,' agreed Julian. 'We shall have plenty of time to have a word with Nobby, and to find a good camping-place before night comes – and to find a farm, too, that will let us have food. Won't Nobby be surprised to see us?'

They cleared up, put the horses into their harness again and set off for the circus camp. Now for a bit of excitement!

Chapter Six

THE CIRCUS CAMP AND NOBBY

IT did not take the caravans very long to come in sight of the circus camp. As George had said, it was in a comfortable hollow, set at the foot of the hills – a quiet spot, well away from any dwelling-places, where the circus animals could enjoy a certain amount of freedom and be exercised in peace.

The caravans were set round in a wide circle. Tents had been put up here and there. The big elephant was tied by a thick rope to a stout tree. Dogs ran about everywhere, and a string of shining horses was being paraded round a large field nearby.

'There they all are!' said Anne, excitedly, standing up on the driving-seat to see better. 'Golly, the chimpanzee is loose, isn't he? No, he isn't – someone has got him on a rope. Is it Nobby with him?'

'Yes, it is. I say, fancy walking about with a live chimp like that!' said Julian.

The children looked at everything with the greatest interest as their caravans came nearer to the circus camp. Few people seemed to be about that hot afternoon. Nobby was there with the chimpanzee, and one or two women were stirring pots over small fires – but that seemed to be all.

The circus dogs set up a great barking as the red and green caravans drew nearer. One or two men came out of the tents and looked up the track that led to the camp.

They pointed to the children's caravans and seemed astonished.

Nobby, with the chimpanzee held firmly by the paw, came out of the camp in curiosity to meet the strange caravans. Julian hailed him.

'Hi, Nobby! You didn't think you'd see *us* here, did you?'

Nobby was amazed to hear his name called. At first he did not remember the children at all. Then he gave a yell.

'Jumping Jiminy, it's you kids I saw away back on the road! What are *you* doing here?'

Timmy growled ominously and George called to Nobby. 'He's never seen a chimpanzee before. Do you think they'll be friends?'

'Don't know,' said Nobby doubtfully. 'Old Pongo likes the circus dogs all right. Anyway, don't you let your dog fly at Pongo, or he'll be eaten alive! A chimp is very strong, you know.'

'Could I make friends with Pongo, do you think?' asked George. 'If he would shake hands with me, or something, Timmy would know I was friends with him and he'd be all right. Would Pongo make friends with me?'

' 'Course he will!' said Nobby. 'He's the sweetest-tempered chimp alive – ain't you, Pongo? Now, shake hands with the lady.'

Anne didn't feel at all inclined to go near the chimpanzee, but George was quite fearless. She walked up to the big animal and held out her hand. The chimpanzee took it at once, raised it to his mouth and pretended to nibble it, making friendly noises all the time.

George laughed. 'He's nice, isn't he?' she said. 'Timmy, this is Pongo, a friend. Nice Pongo, good Pongo!'

She patted Pongo on the shoulder to show Timmy that she liked the chimpanzee, and Pongo at once patted her on the shoulder, too, grinning amiably. He then patted her on the head and pulled one of her curls.

Timmy wagged his tail a little. He looked very doubtful indeed. What was this strange creature that his mistress appeared to like so much. He took a step towards Pongo.

'Come on, Timmy, say how do you do to Pongo,' said George. 'Like this.' And she shook hands with the chimpanzee again. This time he wouldn't let her hand go, but went on shaking it up and down as if he was pumping water with a pump-handle.

'He won't let go,' said George.

'Don't be naughty, Pongo,' said Nobby in a stern voice. Pongo at once dropped George's hand and covered his face with a hairy paw as if he was ashamed. But the children saw that he was peeping through his fingers with wicked eyes that twinkled with fun.

'He's a real monkey!' said George, laughing.

'You're wrong – he's an ape!' said Nobby. 'Ah, here comes Timmy to make friends. Jumping Jiminy, they're shaking paws!'

So they were. Timmy, having once made up his mind that Pongo was to be a friend, remembered his manners and held out his right paw as he had been taught. Pongo seized it and shook it vigorously. Then he walked round to the back of Timmy and shook hands with his tail. Timmy didn't know what to make of it all.

The children yelled with laughter, and Timmy sat down firmly on his tail. Then he stood up again, his tail wagging, for Barker and Growler had come rushing up. Timmy remembered them, and they remembered him.

'Well, *they're* making friends all right,' said Nobby, pleased. 'Now they'll introduce Timmy to all the other dogs, and there'll be no trouble. Hey, look out for Pongo, there!'

The chimpanzee had stolen round to the back of Julian and was slipping his hand into the boy's pocket.

Nobby went to him and slapped the chimpanzee's paw hard.

'Naughty! Bad boy! Pickpocket!'

The children laughed again when the chimpanzee covered his face with his paws, pretending to be ashamed.

'You'll have to watch out when Pongo's about,' said Nobby. 'He loves to take things out of people's pockets. I say – do tell me – are those your caravans? Aren't they posh?'

'They've been lent to us,' said Dick. 'As a matter of fact, it was seeing your circus go by, with all its gay caravans, that made us think of borrowing caravans, too, and coming away for a holiday.'

'And as you'd told us where you were going we thought we'd follow you and find you out, and get you to show us round the camp,' said Julian. 'Hope you don't mind.'

'I'm proud,' said Nobby, going a bright red. ' 'Tisn't often folks want to make friends with a circus fellow like me – not gentlefolk like you, I mean. I'll be proud to show you round – and you can make friends with every blessed monkey, dog and horse on the place!'

'Oh, thanks!' said all four at once.

'Jolly decent of you,' said Dick. 'Gosh, look at that chimp – he's trying to shake hands with Timmy's tail again. I bet he's funny in the circus ring, ·isn't he, Nobby?'

'He's a scream,' said Nobby. 'Brings the house down. You should see him act with my Uncle Dan. He's the chief clown, you know. Pongo is just as big a clown as my uncle is – it's a fair scream to see them act the fool together.'

'I wish we *could* see them,' said Anne. 'Acting in the

ring, I mean. Will your uncle mind you showing us all the animals and everything?'

'Why should he?' said Nobby. 'Shan't ask him! But you'll mind and act polite to him, won't you? He's worse than a tiger when he's in a temper. They call him Tiger Dan because of his rages.'

Anne didn't like the sound of that at all – Tiger Dan! It sounded very fierce and savage.

'I hope he isn't about anywhere now,' she said nervously, looking round.

'No. He's gone off somewhere,' said Nobby. 'He's a lonesome sort of chap – got no friends much in the circus, except Lou, the acrobat. That's Lou over there.'

Lou was a long-limbed, loose-jointed fellow with an ugly face, and a crop of black shining hair that curled tightly. He sat on the steps of a caravan, smoking a pipe and reading a paper. The children thought that he and Tiger Dan would make a good pair – bad-tempered, scowling and unfriendly. They all made up their minds that they would have as little as possible to do with Lou the acrobat and Tiger Dan the clown.

'Is he a very good acrobat?' said Anne in a low voice, though Lou was much too far away to hear her.

'Fine. First class,' said Nobby with admiration in his voice. 'He can climb anything anywhere – he could go up that tree there like a monkey – and I've seen him climb a drainpipe straight up the side of a tall building just like a cat. He's a marvel. You should see him on the tight-rope, too. He can dance on it!'

The children gazed at Lou with awe. He felt their glances, looked up and scowled. 'Well,' thought Julian, 'he may be the finest acrobat that ever lived – but he's a jolly nasty-looking fellow. There's not much to choose between him and Tiger Dan!'

Lou got up, uncurling his long body like a cat. He moved easily and softly. He loped to Nobby, still with the ugly scowl on his face.

'Who are these kids?' he said. 'What are they doing messing about here?'

'We're not messing about,' said Julian politely. 'We came to see Nobby. We've seen him before.'

Lou looked at Julian as if he was something that smelt nasty. 'Them your caravans?' he asked jerking his head towards them.

'Yes,' said Julian.

'Posh, aren't you?' said Lou sneeringly.

'Not particularly,' said Julian, still polite.

'Any grown-ups with you?' asked Lou.

'No. I'm in charge,' said Julian, 'and we've got a dog that flies at people he doesn't like.'

Timmy clearly didn't like Lou. He stood near him, growling in his throat. Lou kicked out at him.

George caught hold of Timmy's collar just in time. 'Down Tim, down!' she cried. Then she turned on Lou, her eyes blazing.

'Don't you dare kick my dog!' she shouted. 'He'll have you down on the ground if you do. You keep out of his way, or he'll go for you now.'

Lou spat on the ground in contempt and turned to go. 'You clear out,' he said. 'We don't want no kids messing about here. And I ain't afraid of no dog. I got ways of dealing with bad dogs.'

'What do you mean by that?' yelled George, still in a furious temper. But Lou did not bother to reply. He went up the steps of his caravan and slammed the door shut. Timmy barked angrily and tugged at his collar, which George was still holding firmly.

'Now you've torn it!' said Nobby dismally. 'If Lou catches you about anywhere he'll hoof you out. And you be careful of that dog of yours, or he'll disappear.'

George was angry and alarmed. 'Disappear! What do you mean? If you think Timmy would let anyone steal him, you're wrong.'

'All right, all right. I'm only telling you. Don't fly at me like that!' said Nobby. 'Jumping Jiminy, look at that chimp. He's gone inside one of your caravans!'

The sudden storm was forgotten as everyone rushed to the green caravan. Pongo was inside, helping himself liberally from a tin of sweets. As soon as he saw the children he groaned and covered his face with his paws – but he sucked hard at the sweets all the time.

'Pongo! Bad boy! Come here!' scolded Nobby. 'Shall I whip you?'

'Oh, no, don't,' begged Anne. 'He's a scamp, but I do like him. We've plenty of sweets to spare. You have some, too, Nobby.'

'Well, thank you.' said Nobby, and helped himself. He grinned round at everyone. 'Nice to have friends like you,' he said. 'Ain't it, Pongo?'

Chapter Seven

A TEA-PARTY – AND A VISIT IN THE NIGHT

NOBODY particularly wanted to see round the camp just then, as Lou had been so unpleasant. So instead they showed the admiring Nobby over the two caravans. He had never seen such beauties.

'Jumping Jiminy, they're like palaces!' he said. 'Do you mean to say them taps turn on and water comes out? Can I turn on a tap? I've never turned a tap in my life!'

He turned the taps on and off a dozen times, exclaiming in wonder to see the water come gushing out. He thumped the bunks to see how soft they were. He admired the gay soft rugs and the shining crockery. He was, in fact, a very nice guest to have, and the children liked him more and more. They liked Barker and Growler, too, who were both well-behaved, obedient, merry dogs.

Pongo, of course, wanted to turn the taps on and off, too, and he threw all the coverings off the two bunks to see what was underneath. He also took the kettle off the stove put the spout to his thick lips and drank all the water out of it very noisily indeed.

'You're forgetting your manners, Pongo!' said Nobby in horror, and snatched the kettle away from him. Anne squealed with laughter. She loved the chimpanzee, and he seemed to have taken a great fancy to Anne, too. He followed her about and stroked her hair and made funny affectionate noises.

'Would you like to stay and have tea here with us?'

asked Julian, looking at his watch. 'It's about time.'

'Coo – I don't have tea as a rule,' said Nobby. 'Yes, I'd like to. Sure you don't mind me staying, though? I ain't got your manners, I know, and I'm a bit dirty, and not your sort at all. But you're real kind.'

'We'd love to have you stay,' said Anne in delight. 'I'll cut some bread and butter and make some sandwiches. Do you like potted meat sandwiches, Nobby?'

'Don't I just!' said Nobby. 'And Pongo does, too. Don't you let him get near them or he'll finish up the lot.'

It was a pleasant and amusing little tea-party. They all sat out on the heather, on the shady side of the caravan. Barker and Growler sat with Timmy. Pongo sat beside Anne, taking bits of sandwich from her most politely. Nobby enjoyed his tea immensely, eating more sandwiches than anyone and talking all the time with his mouth full.

He made the four children yell with laughter. He imitated his Uncle Dan doing some of his clown tricks. He turned cart-wheels all round the caravan while he was waiting for Anne to cut more sandwiches. He stood solemnly on his head and ate a sandwich like that, much to Timmy's amazement. Timmy walked round and round him, and sniffed at his face as if to say: 'Strange! No legs! Something's gone wrong.'

At last nobody could eat any more. Nobby stood up to go, suddenly wondering if he had stayed too long.

'I was enjoying myself so much I forgot the time,' he said awkwardly. 'Bet I've stayed too long and you've been too polite to tell me to get out. Coo, that wasn't half a good tea! Thanks, Miss, awfully, for all them delicious sandwiches. 'Fraid my manners aren't like yours, kids, but thanks for a very good time.'

'You've got very good manners indeed,' said Anne, warmly. 'You've been a splendid guest. Come again, won't you?'

'Well, thanks, I will,' said Nobby, forgetting his sudden awkwardness, and beaming round. 'Where's Pongo? Look at that chimp! He's got one of your hankies, and he's blowing his nose!'

Anne squealed in delight. 'He can keep it!' she said. 'It's only an old one.'

'Will you be here camping for long?' asked Nobby.

'Well, not just exactly *here*,' said Julian. 'We thought of going up higher into the hills. It will be cooler there. But we might camp here just for tonight. We meant to go up higher this evening, but we might as well stay here and go tomorrow morning now. Perhaps we could see round the camp tomorrow morning.'

'Not if Lou's there you can't,' said Nobby. 'Once he's told people to clear out he means it. But it will be all right if he's not. I'll come and tell you.'

'All right,' said Julian. 'I'm not afraid of Lou – but we don't want to get *you* into any trouble, Nobby. If Lou's there tomorrow morning, we'll go on up into the hills, and you can always signal to us if he's out of the camp, and we can come down any time. And mind you come up and see us when you want to.'

'And bring Pongo,' said Anne.

'You bet!' said Nobby. 'Well – so long!'

He went off with Barker and Growler at his heels and with Pongo held firmly by the paw. Pongo didn't want to go at all. He kept pulling back like a naughty child.

'I do like Nobby and Pongo,' said Anne. 'I wonder what Mummy would say if she knew we'd made friends with a chimpanzee. She'd have a fit.'

Julian suddenly looked rather doubtful. He was wondering if he had done right to follow the circus and let

Anne and the others make friends with such queer folk and even queerer animals. But Nobby was so nice. He was sure his mother would like Nobby. And they could easily keep away from Tiger Dan and Lou the acrobat.

'Have we got enough to eat for supper tonight and breakfast tomorrow?' he asked Anne. 'Because there doesn't seem to be a farm near enough to go to just here. But Nobby says there's one up on the hill up there – the circus folk get their supplies from it, too – what they don't get from the nearest town. Apparently somebody goes in each day to shop.'

'I'll just see what we've got in the larder, Julian,' said Anne, getting up. She knew perfectly well what there was in the larder – but it made her feel grown-up and important to go and look. It was nice to feel like that when she so often felt small and young, and the others were big and knew so much.

She called back to them: 'I've got eggs and tomatoes and potted meat, and plenty of bread, and a cake we bought today, and a pound of butter.'

'That's all right then,' said Julian. 'We won't bother about going to the farm tonight.'

When darkness fell that night, there were clouds across the sky for the first time. Not a star showed and there was no moon. It was pitch-black, and Julian, looking out of the window of his caravan, before clambering into his bunk, could not even see a shimmer of water from the lake.

He got into his bunk and pulled the covers up. In the other caravan George and Anne were asleep. Timmy was, as usual, on George's feet. She had pushed him off them once or twice, but now that she was asleep he was

undisturbed, and lay heavily across her ankles, his head
on his paws.

Suddenly his ears cocked up. He raised his head cautiously. Then he growled softly in his throat. He had heard
something. He sat there stiffly, listening. He could hear
footsteps from two different directions. Then he heard
voices – cautious voices, low and muffled.

Timmy growled again, more loudly. George awoke
and reached for his collar. 'What's the matter?' she
whispered. Timmy listened and so did she. They both
heard the voices.

George slipped quietly out of the bunk and went to the
half-open door of the caravan. She could not see anything outside at all because it was so dark. 'Don't make
a noise, Tim,' she whispered.

Timmy understood. He did not growl again, but
George could feel the hairs rising all along the back of his
neck.

The voices seemed to come from not very far away.
Two men must be talking together, George thought.
Then she heard a match struck, and in its light she saw
two men lighting their cigarettes from the same match.
She recognised them at once – they were Nobby's Uncle
Dan and Lou the acrobat.

What were they doing there? Had they got a meeting-
place there – or had they come to steal something from
the caravans? George wished she could tell Julian and
Dick – but she did not like to go out of her caravan in
case the men heard her.

At first she could not hear anything the men said. They
were discussing something very earnestly. Then one
raised his voice.

'Okay, then – that's settled.' Then came the sound of footsteps again, this time towards George's caravan. The men walked straight into the side of it, exclaimed in surprise and pain, and began to feel about to find out what they had walked into.

'It's those posh caravans!' George heard Lou exclaim. 'Still here! I told those kids to clear out!'

'What kids?' asked Tiger Dan, in surprise. Evidently he had come back in the dark and did not know they had arrived.

'Some kids Nobby knows,' said Lou in an angry voice. He rapped loudly on the walls of the caravan, and Anne woke up with a jump. George, just inside the caravan with Timmy, jumped in fright, too. Timmy barked in rage.

Julian and Dick woke up. Julian flashed on his torch and went to his door. The light picked out the two men standing by George's caravan.

'What are you doing here at this time of night?' said Julian. 'Making a row like that! Clear off!'

This was quite the wrong thing to have said to Dan and Lou, both bad-tempered men who felt that the whole of the camping-ground around belonged to them and the circus.

'Who do you think you're talking to?' shouted Dan angrily. 'You're the ones to clear off! Do you hear?'

'Didn't I tell you to clear out this afternoon?' yelled Lou, losing his temper, too. 'You do as you're told, you young rogue, or I'll set the dogs on you and have you chased for miles.'

Anne began to cry. George trembled with rage. Timmy growled. Julian spoke calmly but determinedly.

'We're going in the morning, as we meant. But if you're suggesting we should go now, you can think again. This is as much our camping-ground as yours. Now get off, and don't come disturbing us again.'

'I'll give you a leathering, you young cockerel!' cried Lou, and began to unfasten the leather belt from round his waist.

George let go her hold of Timmy's collar. 'Go for them, Timmy,' she said. 'But don't bite. Just worry them!'

Timmy sprang down to the ground with a joyful bark. He flung himself at the two men. He knew what George wanted him to do, and although he longed to snap at the two rogues with his sharp teeth, he didn't. He pretended to, though, and growled so fiercely that they were scared out of their wits.

Lou hit out at Timmy, threatening to kill him. But Timmy cared for no threats of that kind. He got hold of Lou's right trouser-leg, pulled, and ripped it open from knee to ankle.

'Come on – the dog's mad!' cried Dan. 'He'll have us by the throat if we don't go. Call him off, you kids. We're going. But mind you clear out in the morning, or we'll see you do! We'll pay you out one day.'

Seeing that the men really meant to go, George whistled to Timmy. 'Come here, Tim. Stand on guard till they're really gone. Fly at them if they come back.'

But the men soon disappeared – and nothing would have made either of them come back and face Timmy again that night!

Chapter Eight

UP IN THE HILLS

THE four children were upset and puzzled by the behaviour of the two men. George told how Timmy had wakened her by growling and how she had heard the men talking together in low voices.

'I don't really think they had come to steal anything,' she said. 'I think they were just meeting near here for a secret talk. They didn't know the caravans were here and walked straight into ours.'

'They're bad-tempered brutes,' said Julian. 'And I don't care what you say, George, I'm going to lock your caravan door tonight. I know you've got Timmy – but I'm not running any risk of these men coming back, Timmy or no Timmy.'

Anne was so scared that George consented to let Julian lock the red caravan door. Timmy was locked in with them. The boys went back to their own caravan, and Julian locked his door, too, from the inside. He wanted to be on the safe side.

'I'll be glad to get away from here up into the hills,' he said. 'I shan't feel safe as long as we are quite so near the camp. We'll be all right up in the hills.'

'We'll go first thing after breakfast,' said Dick, settling down to his bunk again. 'Gosh, it's a good thing the girls had Timmy tonight. Those fellows looked as if they meant to go for you properly, Ju.'

'Yes. I shouldn't have had much chance against the

two of them either,' said Julian. 'They are both hefty, strong fellows.'

The next morning all the four awoke early. Nobody felt inclined to lie and snooze – all of them were anxious to get off before Lou and Dan appeared again.

'You get the breakfast, Anne and George, and Dick and I will catch the horses and put them in the caravan shafts,' said Julian. 'Then we shall be ready to go off immediately after breakfast.'

They had breakfast and cleared up. They got up on to the driving-seats and were just about to drive away when Lou and Dan came down the track towards them.

'Oh, you're going, are you?' said Dan, with an ugly grin on his face. 'That's right. Nice to see kids so obedient. Where you going?'

'Up into the hills,' said Julian. 'Not that it's anything to do with you where we go.'

'Why don't you go round the foot of the hills, instead of over the top?' said Lou. 'Silly way to go – up there, with the caravans dragging them horses back all the way.'

Julian was just about to say that he didn't intend to go right up to the top of the hills and over to the other side, when he stopped himself. No – just as well not to let these fellows know that he meant to camp up there, or they might come and worry them all again.

He clicked to Dobby. 'We're going the way we want to go,' he said to Lou in a curt voice. 'And that's up the hill. Get out of the way, please.'

As Dobby was walking straight at them, the men had to jump to one side. They scowled at the four children. Then they all heard the sound of running footsteps and along came Nobby, with Barker and Growler at his heels as usual.

'Hey, what you going so early for?' he yelled. 'Let me come part of the way with you.'

'No, you don't,' said his uncle, and gave the surprised boy an unexpected cuff. 'I've told these kids to clear out, and they're going. I won't have no meddling strangers round this camp. And don't you kid yourself they want to make friends with you, see! You go and get out those dogs and exercise them, or I'll give you another box on the ears that'll make you see all the stars in the sky.'

Nobby stared at him, angry and afraid. He knew his uncle too well to defy him. He turned on his heel sullenly and went off back to the camp. The caravans overtook him on the way. Julian called to him in a low voice:

'Cheer up, Nobby. We'll be waiting for you up in the hills – don't tell Lou and your uncle about it. Let them think we've gone right away. Bring Pongo up sometime!'

Nobby grinned. 'Right you are!' he said. 'I can bring the dogs up to exercise them, too – but not today. I dursent today. And as soon as them two are safely out for the day I'll bring you down to the camp and show you round, see? That all right?'

'Fine,' said Julian, and drove on. Neither Lou nor Dan had heard a word, or even guessed that this conversation was going on, for Nobby had been careful to walk on all the time and not even turn his face towards the children.

The road wound upwards into the hills. At first it was not very steep, but wound to and fro across the side of the hill. Half-way up the caravans crossed a stone bridge under which a very swift stream flowed.

'That stream's in a hurry!' said George, watching it bubble and gurgle downwards. 'Look – is that where it starts from – just there in the hillside?'

She pointed some way up the hill, and it seemed as if the stream really did suddenly start just where she pointed.

'But it can't suddenly start there – not such a big fast stream as this!' said Julian, stopping Dobby on the other side of the bridge. 'Let's go and see, I'm thirsty, and if there's a spring there, it will be very cold and clear – lovely to drink from. Come on, we'll go and see.'

But there was no spring. The stream did not 'begin' just there, but flowed out of a hole in the hillside, as big and as fast as it was just under the stone bridge. The children bent down and peered into the water-filled hole.

'It comes out from inside the hill,' said Anne, surprised. 'Fancy it running around in the hill itself. It must be glad to find a way out!'

They didn't like to drink it as it was not the clear, fresh spring they had hoped to find. But, wandering a little farther on, they came to a real spring that gushed out from beneath a stone, cold and crystal clear. They drank from this and voted that it was the nicest drink they had ever had in their lives. Dick followed the spring-water downwards and saw that it joined the little rushing stream.

'I suppose it flows into the lake,' he said. 'Come on. Let's get on and find a farm, Julian. I'm sure I heard the crowing of a cock just then, so one can't be far away.'

They went round a bend of the hill and saw the farm, a rambling collection of old buildings sprawling down the hillside. Hens ran about, clucking. Sheep grazed

above the farm, and cows chewed the cud in fields
nearby. A man was working not far off, and Julian
hailed him. 'Good morning! Are you the farmer?'

'No. Farmer's over yonder,' said the man, pointing
to a barn near the farm house. 'Be careful of the dogs.'

The two caravans went on towards the farm. The
farmer heard them coming and came out with his dogs.
When he saw that there were only children driving the
two caravans he looked surprised.

Julian had a polite, well-mannered way with him that
all the grown-ups liked. Soon he was deep in a talk with
the man, with most satisfactory results. The farmer was
willing to supply them with any farm produce they
wanted, and they could have as much milk as they liked
at any time. His wife, he was sure, would cook them
anything they asked her to, and bake them cakes, too.

'Perhaps I could arrange payment with her?' said
Julian. 'I'd like to pay for everything as I buy it.'

'That's right, son,' said the farmer. 'Always pay your
way as you go along, and you won't come to any harm.
You go and see my old woman. She likes children and
she'll make you right welcome. Where are you going to
camp?'

'I'd like to camp somewhere with a fine view over the
lake,' said Julian. 'We can't see it from just here. Maybe
a bit farther on we'll get just the view I want.'

'Yes, you go on about half a mile,' said the farmer.
'The track goes that far – and when you come to a clump
of fine birch trees you'll see a sheltered hollow, set right
in the hillside, with a wonderful fine view over the lake.
You can pull your caravans in there, son, and you'll be
sheltered from the winds.'

'Thanks awfully,' said all the children together, thinking what a nice man this old farmer was. How different from Lou and Dan, with their threats and rages!

'We'll go and see your wife first, sir,' said Julian. 'Then we'll go on and pull into the hollow you suggest. We'll be seeing you again some time, I expect.'

They went to see the farmer's wife, a fat, round-cheeked old woman, whose little curranty eyes twinkled with good humour. She made them very welcome, gave them hot buns from the oven and told them to help themselves to the little purple plums on the tree outside the old farm house.

Julian arranged to pay on the spot for anything they bought each day. The prices the farmer's wife asked seemed very low indeed, but she would not hear of taking any more money for her goods.

'It'll be a pleasure to see your bonny faces at my door!' she said. 'That'll be part of my payment, see? I can tell you're well-brought-up children by your nice manners and ways. You'll not be doing any damage or foolishness on the farm, *I* know.'

The children came away laden with all kinds of food, from eggs and ham to scones and ginger cakes. She pushed a bottle of raspberry syrup into Anne's hand when the little girl said good-bye. But when Julian turned back to pay her for it she was quite annoyed.

'If I want to make a present to somebody I'll do it!' she said. 'Go on with you . . . paying for this and paying for that. I'll have a little something extra for you each time, and don't you dare to ask to pay for it, or I'll be after you with my rolling pin!'

'Isn't she awfully nice?' said Anne as they made their

way back to the caravans. 'Even Timmy offered to shake
hands with her without you telling him to, George – and
he hardly ever does that to anyone, does he?'

They packed the things away into the larder, got up
into the driving-seats, clicked to Dobby and Trotter and
set off up the track again.

Just over half a mile away was a clump of birch trees.
'We'll find that sheltered hollow near them,' said Julian.

'Yes, look – there it is – set back into the hill, a really
cosy place! Just right for camping in – and oh, what a
magnificent view!'

It certainly was. They could see right down the steep
hillside to the lake. It lay spread out, flat and smooth,
like an enchanted mirror. From where they were they
could now see right to the opposite banks of the lake – and
it was indeed a big stretch of water.

'Isn't it blue?' said Anne, staring. 'Bluer even than the
sky. Oh, won't it be lovely to see this marvellous view
every single day we're here?'

Julian backed the caravans into the hollow. Heather
grew there, like a springy purple carpet. Harebells, pale
as an evening sky, grew in clumps in crevices of the hill
behind. It was a lovely spot for camping in.

George's sharp ears caught the sound of water and she
went to look for it. She called back to the others. 'What
do you think? There's another spring here, coming out of
the hill. Drinking and washing water laid on! Aren't we
lucky?'

'We certainly are,' said Julian. 'It's a lovely place –
and nobody will disturb us here!'

But he spoke too soon!

Chapter Nine

AN UNPLEASANT MEETING

IT really was fun settling into that cosy hollow. The two caravans were backed in side by side. The horses were taken out and led to a big field where the farmer's horses were kept when they had done their day's work. Trotter and Dobby seemed very pleased with the green, sloping field. It had a spring of its own that ran into a stone trough and out of it, keeping it always filled with fresh cold water. Both horses went to take a long drink.

'Well, that settles the two horses all right,' said Julian. 'We'll tell the farmer he can borrow them if he wants to – he'll be harvesting soon and may like to have Dobby and Trotter for a few days. They will enjoy hobnobbing with other horses again.'

At the front of the hollow was a rocky ledge, hung with heathery tufts. 'This is the front seat for Lake View!' said Anne. 'Oh, it's warm from the sun! How lovely!'

'I vote we have all our meals on this ledge,' said George, sitting down too. 'It's comfortable and roomy – and flat enough to take our cups and plates without spilling anything – and honestly the view from here is too gorgeous for words. Can anyone see anything of the circus from up here?'

'There's a spire or two of smoke over yonder,' said Dick, pointing. 'I should think that's where the camp is. And look – there's a boat pushing out on the lake – doesn't it look tiny?'

'Perhaps Nobby is in it,' said Anne. 'Haven't we brought any field-glasses, Julian? I thought we had.'

'Yes – we have,' said Julian, remembering. 'I'll get them.' He went to the green caravan, rummaged about in the drawers, and came out with his field-glasses swinging on the end of their straps.

'Here we are!' he said, and set them to his eyes. 'Yes – I can see the boat clearly now – and it *is* Nobby in it – but who's with him? Golly, it's Pongo!'

Everyone had to look through the glasses to see Nobby and Pongo in the boat. 'You know, we could always get Nobby to signal to us somehow from his boat when he wanted to tell us that Lou and his uncle were away,' said Dick. 'Then we should know it was safe, and we could pop down to the camp and see round it.'

'Yes. Good idea,' said George. 'Give me the glasses, Dick. Timmy wants to have a turn at seeing, too.'

'He can't see through glasses like these, idiot,' said Dick, handing them to George. But Timmy most solemnly glued his eyes to the glasses, and appeared to be looking through them very earnestly indeed.

'Woof,' he remarked, when he took his eyes away at last.

'He says he's seen Nobby and Pongo, too,' said George, and the others laughed. Anne half-believed that he had. Timmy was such an extraordinary dog, she thought, as she patted his smooth head.

It was a terribly hot day. Too hot to do anything – even to walk down to the lake and bathe! The children were glad they were up in the hills, for at least there was a little breeze that fanned them now and again. They did not expect to see Nobby again that day, but they hoped he would come up the next day. If not they would go down and bathe in the lake and hope to see him somewhere about there.

Soon the rocky ledge got too hot to sit on. The children retreated to the clump of birch trees, which at least cast some shade. They took books with them, and Timmy came along, too, panting as if he had run for miles. He kept going off to the little spring to drink. Anne filled a big bowl with the cold water, and stood it in a breezy place near by, with a cup to dip into it. They were thirsty all day long, and it was pleasant to dip a cup into the bowl of spring-water and drink.

The lake was unbelievably blue that day, and lay as still as a mirror. Nobby's boat was no longer in the water. He and Pongo had gone. There was not a single movement to be seen down by the lake.

'Shall we go down to the lake this evening, when it's cooler, and bathe there?' said Julian, at tea-time. 'We haven't had much exercise today, and it would do us good to walk down and have a swim. We won't take Timmy in case we happen to come across Lou or Dan. He'd certainly fly at them today. We can always keep an eye open for those two and avoid them ourselves – but Timmy would go for them as soon as he spotted them. We might be in the water and unable to stop him.'

'Anyway, he'll guard the caravans for us,' said Anne. 'Well, I'll just take these cups and plates and rinse them in the stream. Nobody wants any more to eat, do they?'

'Too hot,' said Dick, rolling over on to his back. 'I wish we were by the lake at this moment – I'd go straight into the water now!'

At half-past six it was cooler, and the four children set

off down the hill. Timmy was angry and hurt at being left behind.

'You're to be on guard, Timmy,' said George firmly. 'See? Don't let anyone come near our caravans. On guard, Timmy!'

'Woof,' said Timmy dismally, and put his tail down. On guard! Didn't George know that the caravans wouldn't walk off by themselves, and that he wanted a good splash in the lake?

Still, he stayed behind, standing on the rocky ledge to see the last of the children, his ears cocked to hear their voices and his tail still down in disgust. Then he went and lay down beneath George's caravan, and waited patiently for his friends to return.

The children went down the hill with their bathing-things, taking short cuts, and leaping like goats over the steep bits. It had seemed quite a long way up when they had gone so slowly in the caravans with Dobby and Trotter – but it wasn't nearly so far when they could go on their own legs, and take rabbit-paths and short cuts whenever they liked.

There was one steep bit that forced them back on to the track. They went along it to where the track turned a sharp corner round a cliff-like bend – and to their surprise and dismay they walked almost straight into Lou and Tiger Dan!

'Take no notice,' said Julian, in a low voice. 'Keep together and walk straight on. Pretend that Timmy is somewhere just behind us.'

'Tim, Tim!' called George, at once.

Lou and Dan seemed just as surprised to see the children, as they had been to see the two men. They stopped and looked hard at them, but Julian hurried the others on.

'Hey, wait a minute!' called Dan. 'I thought you had gone off – over the hill-top!'

'Sorry we can't stop!' called back Julian. 'We're in rather a hurry!'

Lou looked round for Timmy. He wasn't going to lose his temper and start shouting in case that mad dog came at him again. He spoke to the children loudly, forcing himself to appear good-tempered.

'Where are your caravans? Are you camping up here anywhere?'

But the children still walked on, and the men had to go after them to make them hear.

'Hey! What's the matter? We shan't hurt you! We only want to know if you're camping here. It's better down below, you know.'

'Keep on walking,' muttered Julian. 'Don't tell them anything. Why do they tell us it's better to camp down below when they were so anxious for us to clear out yesterday? They're mad!'

'Timmy, Timmy!' called George, again, hoping that the men would stop following them if they heard her calling for her dog.

It did stop them. They gave up going after the children, and didn't shout any more. They turned angrily and went on up the track.

'Well, we've thrown them off all right,' said Dick, with relief. 'Don't look so scared, Anne. I wonder what they want up in the hills. They don't look the sort that would go walking for pleasure.'

'Dick – we're not going to have another adventure, are

we?' said Anne suddenly, looking very woebegone. 'I don't want one. I just want a nice ordinary, peaceful holiday.'

' 'Course we're not going to have an adventure!' said Dick, scornfully. 'Just because we meet two bad-tempered fellows from a circus camp you think we're in for an adventure, Anne! Well, *I* jolly well wish we were! Every hols we've been together so far we've had adventures – and you must admit that you love talking about them and remembering them.'

'Yes, I do. But I don't like it much when I'm in the *middle* of one,' said Anne. 'I don't think I'm a very adventurous person, really.'

'No, you're not,' said Julian, pulling Anne over a very steep bit. 'But you're a very nice little person, Anne, so don't worry about it. And, anyway, you wouldn't like to be left out of any of our adventures, would you?'

'Oh *no*,' said Anne. 'I couldn't bear it. Oh, look – we're at the bottom of the hill – and there's the lake, looking icy-cold!'

It wasn't long before they were all in the water – and suddenly there was Nobby too, waving and yelling. 'I'm coming in! Lou and my uncle have gone off somewhere. Hurray!'

Barker and Growler were with Nobby, but not Pongo the chimpanzee. Nobby was soon in the water, swimming like a dog, and splashing George as soon as he got up to her.

'We met Lou and your uncle as we came down,' called George. 'Shut up, Nobby, and let me talk to you. I said, we met Lou and your uncle just now – going up into the hills.'

'Up into the hills?' said Nobby, astonished. 'Whatever for? They don't go and fetch things from the farm. The women do that, early each morning.'

'Well, we met those two,' said Dick swimming up. 'They seemed jolly surprised to see us. I hope they aren't going to bother us any more.'

'I've had a bad day,' said Nobby, and he showed black bruises on his arms. 'My uncle hit me like anything for making friends with you. He says I'm not to go talking to strangers no more.'

'Why ever not?' said Dick. 'What a surly, selfish fellow he is! Well, you don't seem to be taking much notice of him now!'

' 'Course not!' said Nobby. 'He's safe up in the hills, isn't he? I'll have to be careful he doesn't see me with you, that's all. Nobody else at the camp will split on me – they all hate Lou and Tiger Dan.'

'We saw you out in your boat with Pongo,' said Julian, swimming up to join in the conversation. 'We thought that if ever you wanted to signal to us you could easily do it by going out in your boat, and waving a handkerchief or something. We've got field-glasses, and we can easily see you. We could come along down if you signalled. We'd know it would be safe.'

'Right,' said Nobby. 'Come on, let's have a race. Bet you I'm on the shore first!'

He wasn't, of course, because he didn't swim properly. Even Anne could race him. Soon they were all drying themselves vigorously.

'Golly, I'm hungry!' said Julian. 'Come on up the hill with us, Nobby, and share our supper!'

Chapter Ten

A CURIOUS CHANGE OF MIND

NOBBY felt very much tempted to go and have a meal up in the hills with the children. But he was afraid of meeting Lou and his uncle coming back from their walk.

'We can easily look out for them and warn you if we see or hear them,' said Dick, 'and you can flop under a bush and hide till they go past. You may be sure we'll be on the look-out for them ourselves, because *we* don't want to meet them either!'

'Well, I'll come,' said Nobby. 'I'll take Barker and Growler too. They'll like to see Timmy.'

So all five of them, with the two dogs, set off up the hill. They climbed up short cuts at first, but they were soon panting, and decided to take the track, which, although longer, was easier to follow.

They all kept a sharp look-out for the two men, but they could see no sign of them. 'We shall be at our caravans soon,' said Julian. Then he heard Timmy barking in the distance. 'Hallo! What's old Tim barking for? I wonder if those fellows have been up to our caravans?'

'Good thing we left Timmy on guard if so,' said Dick. 'We might have missed something if not.'

Then he went red, remembering that it was Nobby's uncle he had been talking of. Nobby might feel upset and offended to hear someone speaking as if he thought Tiger Dan would commit a little robbery.

But Nobby wasn't at all offended. 'Don't you worry

about what you say of my uncle,' he said, cheerfully. 'He's a bad lot. I know that. Anyway, he's not really my uncle, you know. When my father and mother died, they left a little money for me – and it turned out that they had asked Tiger Dan to look after me. So he took the money, called himself my uncle, and I've had to be with him ever since.'

'Was he in the same circus, then?' asked Julian.

'Oh yes. He and my father were both clowns,' said Nobby. 'Always have been clowns, in my family. But wait till I'm old enough, and I'll do a bunk – clear off and join another circus, where they'll let me look after the horses. I'm mad on horses. But the fellow at our circus won't often let me go near them. Jealous because I can handle them, I suppose!'

The children gazed at Nobby in wonder. He seemed an extraordinary boy to them – one who walked about with a tame chimpanzee, exercised hordes of performing dogs, lived with the chief clown in the circus, could turn the most marvellous cart-wheels, and whose only ambition was to work with horses! What a boy! Dick half-envied him.

'Haven't you ever been to school?' he asked Nobby.

The boy shook his head. 'Never! I can't write. And I can only read a bit. Most circus folk are like that, so nobody minds. Jumping Jiminy, I bet *you're* all clever, though! I bet even little Anne can read a book!'

'I've been able to read for *years*,' said Anne. 'And I'm up to fractions now in numbers.'

'Coo! What's fractions?' said Nobby, impressed.

'Well – quarters and halves and seven-eighths, and things like that,' said Anne. 'But I'd rather be able to turn a cart-wheel like you can, Nobby, than know how to do fractions.'

'Whatever *is* Timmy barking for?' said George as they came near the clump of birch trees. Then she stopped suddenly, for she had seen two figures lying down in the grass below the trees. Lou – and Tiger Dan!

It was too late for Nobby to hide. The men saw him at once. They got up and waited for the children to come near. George felt thankful that Timmy was within whistling distance. He would come at the first call or whistle, she knew.

Julian looked at the men. To his surprise they appeared to be quite amiable. A faint scowl came over Tiger Dan's face when he caught sight of Nobby, but it passed at once.

'Good evening,' said Julian curtly, and would have passed on without another word, but Lou stepped up to him.

'We see you're camping up by here,' said Lou, and smiled showing yellow teeth. 'Ain't you going over the hill?'

'I don't need to discuss my affairs with either you or your friend,' said Julian, sounding extremely grown-up. 'You told us to clear out from down below, and we have. What we do now is nothing to do with you.'

'Ho yes, it is,' said Tiger Dan, sounding as if he was being polite with great difficulty. 'We come up here to-night to plan a place for some of our animals, see? And we don't want you to be in no danger.'

'We shan't be,' said Julian, scornfully. 'And there is plenty of room on these hills for you and your animals and for us, too. You won't scare us off, so don't think it.

We shall stay here as long as we want to – and if we want help there's the farmer and his men quite near by – to say nothing of our dog.'

'Did you leave that there dog on guard?' asked Lou, as he heard Timmy barking again. 'He ought to be destroyed, that dog of yours. He's dangerous.'

'He's only dangerous to rogues and scamps,' said George, joining in at once. 'You keep away from our caravans when Timmy's on guard. He'll maul you if you go near.'

Lou began to lose his temper. 'Well, are you going or ain't you?' he said. 'We've told you we want this here bit of the hill. You can come down and camp by the lake again if you want to.'

'Yes – you come,' said Tiger Dan to the children's growing astonishment. 'You come, see? You can bathe in the lake every day, then – and Nobby here can show you round the camp, and you can make friends with all the animals, see?'

Now it was Nobby's turn to look amazed.

'Jumping Jiminy! Didn't you beat me black and blue for making friends with these kids?' he demanded. 'What's the game, now? You've never had animals up in the hills before. You've . . .'

'Shut up,' said Tiger Dan in such a fierce voice that all the children were shocked. Lou nudged Dan, and he made an effort to appear pleasant again.

'We didn't want Nobby to make friends with posh folk like you,' he began again. 'But it seems as if you want to pal up with him – so it's okay with us. You come on down and camp by the lake, and Nobby'll show you everything in the circus. Can't say fairer than that.'

'You've got other reasons for making all these sugges-
tions,' said Julian, scornfully. 'I'm sorry – but our plans
are made, and I am not going to discuss them with you.'

'Come on,' said Dick. 'Let's go and find Timmy. He's
barking his head off because he can hear us, and it won't
be long before he comes flying along here. Then we
shall find it difficult to keep him off these two fellows.'

The four children began to move off. Nobby looked
doubtfully at his uncle. He didn't know whether to go
with them or not. Lou nudged Dan again.

'You go, too, if you want to,' said Tiger Dan, trying
to grin amiably at the surprised Nobby. 'Keep your fine
friends, see! Much good may they do you!' The grin
vanished into a scowl, and Nobby skipped smartly out of
reach of his uncle's hand. He was puzzled and wondered
what was behind his uncle's change of mind.

He tore after the children. Timmy came to meet them,
barking his head off, waving his plumy tail wildly in joy.

'Good dog, good dog!' said George, patting him. 'You
keep on guard beautifully. You know I would have
whistled for you if I'd wanted you, didn't you, Timmy?
Good dog!'

'I'll get you some supper,' said Anne to everyone.
'We're all famishing. We can talk while we eat. George,
come and help. Julian, can you get some ginger-beer?
And, Dick, do fill up the water-bowl for me.'

The boys winked at one another. They always thought
that Anne was very funny when she took command like
this, and gave her orders. But everyone went obediently
to work.

Nobby went to help Anne. Together they boiled ten
eggs hard in the little saucepan. Then Anne made

tomato sandwiches with potted meat and got out the cake
the farmer's wife had given them. She remembered the
raspberry syrup, too – how lovely!

Soon they were all sitting on the rocky ledge, which
was still warm, watching the sun go down into the lake.
It was a most beautiful evening, with the lake as blue
as a cornflower and the sky flecked with rosy clouds.
They held their hard-boiled eggs in one hand and a
piece of bread and butter in the other, munching happily. There was a dish of salt for everyone to dip their
eggs into.

'I don't know why, but the meals we have on picnics
always taste so much nicer than the ones we have
indoors,' said George. 'For instance, even if we had hard-
boiled eggs and bread and butter indoors, they wouldn't
taste as nice as these.'

'Can everyone eat two eggs?' asked Anne. 'I did two
each. And there's plenty of cake – and more sandwiches and some plums we picked this morning.'

'Best meal I've ever had in my life,' said Nobby, and
picked up his second egg. 'Best company I've ever been
in, too!'

'Thank you,' said Anne, and everyone looked pleased.
Nobby might not have their good manners, but he always
seemed to say just the right thing.

'It's a good thing your uncle didn't make you go back
with him and Lou,' said Dick. 'Funny business –
changing his mind like that!'

They began to talk about it. Julian was very puzzled
indeed, and had even begun to wonder if he hadn't
better find another camping site and go over the hill.

The others raised their voices scornfully.

'JULIAN! We're not cowards. We'll jolly well stay here!'

'What, leave now – why should we? We're in nobody's way, whatever those men say!'

'*I'm* not moving *my* caravan, whatever *anyone* says!' That was George, of course.

'No, don't you go,' said Nobby. 'Don't you take no notice of Lou and my uncle. They can't do nothing to you at all. They're just trying to make trouble for you. You stay and let me show you over the camp, see?'

'It isn't that I *want* to give in to those fellows' ideas,' said Julian. 'It's just that – well, I'm in charge of us all – and I *don't* like the look of Lou and Tiger Dan – and, well . . .'

'Oh, have another egg and forget about it,' said Dick. 'We're going to stay here in this hollow, however much Dan and Lou want us out of it. And, what's more, I'd like to find out why they're so keen to push us off. It seems jolly queer to me.'

The sun went down in a blaze of orange and red, and the lake shimmered with its fiery reflection. Nobby got up regretfully, and Barker and Growler, who had been hobnobbing with Timmy, got up, too.

'I'll have to go,' said Nobby. 'Still got some jobs to do down there. What about you coming down tomorrow to see the animals? You'll like Old Lady, the elephant. She's a pet. And Pongo will be pleased to see you again.'

'Your uncle may have changed his mind again by tomorrow, and not want us near the camp,' said Dick.

'Well – I'll signal to you,' said Nobby. 'I'll go out in the boat, see? And wave a hanky. Then you'll know it's all right. Well – so long! I'll be seeing you.'

Chapter Eleven

FUN AT THE CIRCUS CAMP

NEXT morning, while Anne cleared up the breakfast things with George, and Dick went off to the farm to buy whatever the farmer's wife had ready for him, Julian took the field-glasses and sat on the ledge to watch for Nobby to go out on the lake in his boat.

Dick sauntered along, whistling. The farmer's wife was delighted to see him, and showed him two big baskets full of delicious food.

'Slices of ham I've cured myself,' she said, lifting up the white cloth that covered one of the baskets. 'And a pot of brawn I've made. Keep it in a cool place. And some fresh lettuces and radishes I pulled myself this morning early. And some more tomatoes.'

'How gorgeous!' said Dick, eyeing the food in delight. 'Just the kind of things we love! Thanks awfully, Mrs Mackie. What's in the other basket?'

'Eggs, butter, milk, and a tin of shortbread I've baked,' said Mrs Mackie. 'You should do all right till tomorrow, the four of you! And in that paper there is a bone for the dog.'

'How much do I owe you?' asked Dick. He paid his bill and took up the baskets. Mrs Mackie slipped a bag into his pocket.

'Just a few home-made sweets,' she said. That was her little present. Dick grinned at her.

'Well, I won't offer to pay you for them because I'm

afraid of that rolling-pin of yours,' he said. 'But thank you very, very much.'

He went off delighted. He thought of Anne's pleasure when she came to unpack the baskets. How she would love to put the things in the little larder – and pop the butter in a dish set in a bowl of cold water – and set the eggs in the little rack!

When he got back Julian called to him: 'Nobby's out in his boat. Come and look. He's waving something that can't possibly be a hanky. It must be the sheet off his bed!'

'Nobby doesn't sleep in sheets,' said Anne. 'He didn't know what they were when he saw them in our bunks. Perhaps it's a table-cloth.'

'Anyway, it's something big, to tell us that it's absolutely all right to come down to the camp,' said Julian. 'Are we ready?'

'Not quite,' said Anne, unpacking the baskets Dick had brought. 'I must put away these things – and do you want to take a picnic lunch with you? Because if so I must prepare it. Oh – look at all these gorgeous things!'

They all came back to look. 'Mrs Mackie is a darling,' said Anne. 'Honestly, these things are super – look at this gorgeous ham. It smells heavenly.'

'Here's her little present – home-made sweets,' said Dick, remembering them and taking them out of his pocket. 'Have one?'

Anne had everything ready in half an hour. They had decided to take a picnic lunch with them for themselves and for Nobby as well. They took their bathing-things and towels, too.

'Are we going to take Timmy or not?' said George. 'I

want to. But as these two men seem rather interested in our caravans, perhaps we had better leave him on guard again. We don't want to come back and find the caravans damaged or half the things stolen.'

'I should think not!' said Dick. 'They're not our things, nor our caravans. They belong to somebody else and we've got to take extra good care of them. I think we ought to leave Timmy on guard, don't you, Ju?'

'Yes, I do,' said Julian at once. 'These caravans are too valuable to leave at the mercy of any passing tramp – though I suppose we could lock them up. Anyway – we'll leave Timmy on guard today – poor old Timmy, it's a shame, isn't it?'

Timmy didn't answer. He looked gloomy and miserable. What! They were all going off without him again? He knew what 'on guard' meant – he was to stay here with these houses on wheels till the children chose to come back. He badly wanted to see Pongo again. He stood with his ears and tail drooping, the picture of misery.

But there was no help for it. The children felt that they couldn't leave the caravans unguarded while they were still so uncertain about Lou and Tiger Dan. So they all patted poor Timmy and fondled him, and then said good-bye. He sat down on the rocky ledge with his back to them and wouldn't even watch them go.

'He's sulking,' said George. 'Poor Timothy!'

It didn't take them very long to get down to the camp, and they found Nobby, Pongo, Barker and Growler waiting for them. Nobby was grinning from ear to ear.

'You saw my signal all right?' he said. 'Uncle hasn't changed his mind – in fact, he seems quite to have taken

to you, and says I'm to show you all round and let you
see anything you want to. That was his shirt I waved. I
thought if I waved something enormous you'd know
things were absolutely safe.'

'Where shall we put the bathing-things and the picnic
baskets while we see round the camp?' asked Anne.
'Somewhere cool, if possible.'

'Put them in my caravan,' said Nobby, and led them
to a caravan painted blue and yellow, with red wheels.
The children remembered having seen it when the
procession passed by their house a week or two before.

They peeped inside. It wasn't nearly so nice as theirs.
It was much smaller, for one thing, and very untidy. It
looked dirty, too, and had a nasty smell. Anne didn't
like it very much.

'Not so good as yours!' said Nobby. 'I wish I had a
caravan like yours. I'd feel like a prince. Now what do
you want to see first? The elephant? Come on, then.'

They went to the tree to which Old Lady the elephant
was tied. She curled her trunk round Nobby and looked
at the children out of small, intelligent eyes.

'Well, Old Lady!' said Nobby. 'Want a bathe?'

The elephant trumpeted and made the children jump.
'I'll take you later on,' promised Nobby. 'Now then –
hup, hup, hup!'

At these words the elephant curled her trunk tightly
round Nobby's waist and lifted him bodily into the air,
placing him gently on her big head!

Anne gasped.

'Oh! Did he hurt you, Nobby?'

' 'Course not!' said Nobby. 'Old Lady wouldn't hurt
anyone, would you, big one?'

A small man came up. He had bright eyes that shone as if they had been polished, and a very wide grin. 'Good morning,' he said. 'How do you like my Old Lady? Like to see her play cricket?'

'Oh, *yes*!' said everyone, and the small man produced a cricket bat and held it out to Old Lady. She took it in

her trunk and waved it about. Nobby slipped deftly off
her head to the ground.

'I'll play with her, Larry,' he said, and took the ball
from the small man. He threw it to Old Lady and she
hit it smartly with the bat. It sailed over their heads!

Julian fetched the ball. He threw it at the elephant,
and again the great creature hit the ball with a bang.
Soon all the children were playing with Old Lady and
enjoying the game very much.

Some small camp children came up to watch. But they
were as scared as rabbits as soon as Julian or George
spoke to them and scuttled off to their caravans at once.
They were dirty and ragged, but most of them had
beautiful eyes and thick curly hair, though it wanted
brushing and washing.

Nobby went to fetch Pongo, who was dancing to and
fro in his cage, making anguished sounds, thinking he was
forgotten. He was simply delighted to see the children
again, and put his arm right round Anne at once. Then
he pulled George's hair and hid his face behind his paws,
peeping out mischievously.

'He's a caution, aren't you, Pongo?' said Nobby. 'Now
you keep with me, Pongo, or I'll put you back into your
cage, see?'

They went to see the dogs and let them all out. They
were mostly terrier dogs, or mongrels, smart, well-kept
little things who jumped up eagerly at Nobby, and made
a great fuss of him. It was clear that they loved him and
trusted him.

'Like to see them play football?' asked Nobby. 'Here,
Barker – fetch the ball. Go on, quick!'

Barker darted off to Nobby's caravan. The door was

shut, but the clever little dog stood on his hind legs and jerked the handle with his nose. The door opened and in went Barker. He came out dribbling a football with his nose. Down the steps it went and into the camp field. All the dogs leapt on it with howls of delight.

'Yap-yap-yap! Yap-yap!' They dribbled that football to and fro, while Nobby stood with his legs open to make a goal for them.

It was Barker's job and Growler's to score the goals, and the task of the other dogs to stop them. So it was a most amusing game to watch. Once, when Barker scored a goal by hurling himself on the ball and sending it rolling fast between Nobby's arched legs, Pongo leapt into the fray, picked up the ball and ran off with it.

'Foul, foul!' yelled Nobby and all the dogs rushed after the mischievous chimpanzee. He leapt on to the top of a caravan and began to bounce the ball there, grinning down at the furious dogs.

'Oh, this is such fun!' said Anne, wiping the tears of laughter from her eyes. 'Oh, dear! I've got such a pain in my side from laughing.'

Nobby had to climb up to the roof of the caravan to get the ball. Pongo jumped down the other side, but left the ball balanced neatly on the chimney. He was really a most mischievous chimpanzee.

Then they went to see the beautiful horses. All of them had shining satiny coats. They were being trotted round a big field by a slim, tall young fellow called Rossy, and they obeyed his slightest word.

'Can I ride Black Queen, Rossy?' asked Nobby eagerly. 'Do let me!'

'Okay,' said Rossy, his black hair shining like the horses'

coats. Then Nobby amazed the watching children, for he leapt on to a great black horse, stood up on her back and trotted all round the field like that!

'He'll fall!' cried Anne. But he didn't, of course. Then he suddenly swung himself down on to his hands and rode Black Queen standing upside down.

'Good, good!' cried Rossy. 'You are good with horses, young one! Now ride Fury!'

Fury was a small, fiery-looking little horse, whose gleaming eyes showed a temper. Nobby ran to her and leapt on her bare-backed. She rose up, snorting and tried to throw him off. But he wouldn't be thrown off. No matter what she did, Nobby clung on like a limpet to a rock.

At last Fury tired of it and began to canter round the field. Then she galloped – and suddenly she stopped absolutely dead, meaning to fling Nobby over her head!

But the boy was waiting for that trick and threw himself backwards at once. 'Good, good!' cried Rossy. 'She will soon eat out of your hand, Nobby! Good boy.'

'Nobby, Nobby, you're terribly clever!' yelled Anne. 'Oh, I wish I could do the things you do! I wish I could.'

Nobby slid off Fury's back, looking pleased. It was nice to show off a little to his 'posh' friends. Then he looked round and about. 'I say – where's that chimp? Up to some mischief, I'll be bound! Let's go and find him.'

Chapter Twelve

A LOVELY DAY – WITH A HORRID END

THEY soon saw Pongo. He was coming round one of the caravans, looking exceedingly pleased with himself. He went to Anne and held out his paw to her, making little affectionate noises.

Anne took what he held. She looked at it. 'It's a hard-boiled egg! Oh, Nobby, he's been at the picnic baskets!'

So he had! Two of the eggs were gone, and some of the tomatoes! Nobby smacked the chimpanzee and took him back to his cage. He was very sad and made a noise as if he was crying, hiding his face in his paws. Anne was upset.

'Is he really crying? Oh, do forgive him, Nobby. He didn't mean to be naughty.'

'He's not crying. He's only pretending,' said Nobby. 'And he *did* mean to be naughty. I know him!'

The morning soon went in visiting the circus animals. It was dinner-time before they had had time to see the monkeys. 'We'll see them afterwards,' said Nobby. 'Let's have a meal now. Come on. We'll go and have it by the lake.'

The children hadn't seen Lou or Tiger Dan at all, much to their joy. 'Where are they?' asked Julian. 'Gone out for the day?'

'Yes, thank goodness,' said Nobby. 'Gone out on one of their mysterious jaunts. You know, when we're on the road, going from place to place, my uncle sometimes disappears at night. I wake up – and he's not there.'

'Where does he go?' asked George.

'I wouldn't dare to ask,' said Nobby. 'Anyway, he and Lou are out of the way today. I don't expect they'll be back till night.'

They had their meal by the lake. It glittered at their feet, calm and blue, and looked very inviting.

'What about a swim?' asked Dick when they had eaten as much as they could. Julian looked at his watch.

'Can't swim directly after a good meal,' he said. 'You know that, Dick. We'll have to wait a bit.'

'Right,' said Dick, and lay down. 'I'll have a snooze – or shall we go and see the monkeys?'

They all had a short nap and then got up to go and see the monkeys. When they got back to the camp they found it alive with people, all excited and yelling.

'What's up?' said Nobby. 'Jumping Jiminy, the monkeys are all loose!'

So they were. Wherever they looked the children saw a small brown monkey, chattering to itself, on the roof of a caravan or tent!

A brown-faced woman with sharp eyes came up to Nobby. She caught him by the shoulder and shook him. 'See what that chimp of yours has done!' she said. 'You put him in his cage and couldn't have locked it properly. He got out and let all the monkeys loose. Drat that chimp – I'll take a broomstick to him if ever I catch him!'

'Where's Lucilla then?' asked Nobby, dragging himself away from the cross woman. 'Can't she get them in?'

'Lucilla's gone to the town,' scolded the woman. 'And fine and pleased she'll be to hear this when she comes back!'

'Aw, let the monkeys be!' said Nobby. 'They won't

come to any harm. They'll wait for Lucilla all right!'

'Who's Lucilla?' asked Anne, thinking that life in a circus camp was very exciting.

'She owns the monkeys,' said Nobby. 'Hi, look – there's Lucilla coming back! Now we'll be all right!'

A little wizened old woman was hurrying towards the camp. She really looked rather like a monkey herself, Anne thought. Her eyes were bright and sharp, and her tiny hands clutched a red shawl round her. They looked like brown paws.

'Your monkeys are out!' yelled the camp children. 'LUCILLA! Your monkeys are out.'

Lucilla heard and, raising her voice, she scolded everyone in sight fully and shrilly. Then she stood still and held out her arms. She spoke some soft words in a language the children didn't know – magic words, Anne said afterwards.

One by one the wandering monkeys came scampering over to her, flinging themselves down from the caravan roofs, making little chattering sounds of love and welcome. They leapt on to Lucilla's shoulders and into her arms, cuddling against her like tiny brown children. Not one monkey was left out – all went to Lucilla as if drawn by some enchantment.

She walked slowly towards their cage, murmuring her soft words as she went. Everyone watched in silence.

'She's a queer one,' said the brown-faced woman to Nobby. 'She don't love nobody but her monkeys – and there's nobody loves her but them. You mind out she doesn't go for that chimp of yours, letting out her precious monkeys!'

'I'll take him and Old Lady down to bathe,' said

Nobby, hastily. 'By the time we're back, Lucilla will have forgotten.'

They fetched Old Lady and discovered where naughty Pongo was hiding under a caravan. As quickly as possible they went back to the lake, Old Lady stepping out well, looking forward to her bathe.

'I suppose things like that are always happening in a circus camp,' said Anne. 'It's not a bit like real life.'

'Isn't it?' said Nobby, surprised. 'It's real life all right to *me*!'

It was cool in the lake and they all enjoyed themselves very much, swimming and splashing. Pongo wouldn't go in very far, but splashed everyone who came within reach, laughing and cackling loudly. He gave Old Lady a shock by leaping up on to her back, and pulling one of her big ears.

She dipped her trunk into the lake, sucked up a lot of water, turned her trunk over her back, and squirted the water all over the startled chimpanzee! The children yelled with laughter, and roared again to see Pongo falling in fright off Old Lady's back. Splash! He went right in and got himself wet from head to foot – a thing he hated doing.

'Serves you right, you scamp!' shouted Nobby. 'Hey, Old Lady, stop it! Don't squirt at me!'

The elephant, pleased with her little joke, didn't want to stop it. So the children had to keep well away from her, for her aim was very good.

'I've never had such a lovely time in my life!' said Anne, as she dried herself. 'I shall dream all night of monkeys and elephants, horses, dogs and chimpanzees!'

Nobby turned about twenty cart-wheels by the edge of

the lake from sheer good spirits – and Pongo at once did the same. He was even better at it than Nobby. Anne tried and fell down flop immediately.

They went back to the camp. 'Sorry I can't offer you any tea,' said Nobby, 'but we never seem to have tea, you know – we circus folk, I mean. Anyway, I'm not hungry after that enormous lunch. Are you?'

Nobody was. They shared out Mrs Mackie's home-made toffees, and gave one to Pongo. It stuck his teeth together, and he looked so comically alarmed when he found that he couldn't open his mouth that the children roared at him.

He sat down, swayed from side to side, and began to groan dismally. But the toffee soon melted away, and he found that he could open his mouth after all. He sucked the rest of the sweet noisily, but wouldn't have another.

They wandered round the camp, looking at the different caravans. Nobody took much notice of them now. They were just Nobby's 'posh' friends – that was all. Some of the smaller children peeped out and stuck out their little red tongues – but at Nobby's roar they vanished.

'Got no manners at all!' said Nobby. 'But they're all right really.'

They came to where big wagons stood, stored with all kinds of circus things. 'We don't bother to unpack these when we're resting in camp like this,' said Nobby. 'Don't need them here. One of my jobs is to help to unpack this stuff when we're camping to give a show. Have to get out all them benches and set them up in the big top – that's the circus tent, you know. We're pretty busy then, I can tell you!'

'What's in *this* cart?' asked Anne, coming to a small wagon with a tightly-fitting hood of tarpaulin.

'Don't know,' said Nobby. 'That cart belongs to my uncle. He won't never let me unpack it. I don't know what he keeps there. I've wondered if it was things belonging to my Dad and Mum. I told you they were dead. Anyway, I thought I'd peep and see one day; but Uncle Dan caught me and half-killed me!'

'But if they belonged to your parents, they ought to be yours!' said George.

'Funny thing is, sometimes that cart's crammed full,' said Nobby. 'And sometimes it isn't. Maybe Lou puts some of his things there too.'

'Well, nobody could get anything else in there at the moment!' said Julian. 'It's full to bursting!'

They lost interest in the little wagon and wandered round to see the 'props' as Nobby called them. Anne pictured these as clothes-props, but they turned out to be gilt chairs and tables, the shining poles used for the tight-rope, gaily-painted stools for the performing dogs to sit on, and circus 'props' of that kind.

'*Prop*erties, Anne,' said Julian. 'Circus *prop*erties. Props for short. Look here, isn't it about time we went back? My watch has stopped. Whatever time is it?'

'Golly, it's quite late!' said Dick, looking at his watch. 'Seven o' clock. No wonder I feel jolly hungry. Time we went back. Coming with us, Nobby? You can have supper up there if you like. I bet you could find your way back in the dark.'

'I'll take Pongo with me, and Barker and Growler,' said Nobby, delighted at the invitation. 'If *I* lose the way back, *they* won't!'

So they all set off up the hill, tired with their long and exciting day. Anne began to plan what she would give the little company for supper. Ham, certainly – and tomatoes – and some of that raspberry syrup diluted with icy-cold spring-water.

They all heard Timmy barking excitedly as soon as they came near the caravans. He barked without ceasing, loudly and determinedly.

'He sounds cross,' said Dick. 'Poor old Tim! He must think we've quite deserted him.'

They came to the caravans and Timmy flung himself on George as if he hadn't seen her for a year. He pawed her and licked her, then pawed her again.

Barker and Growler were pleased to see him too, and as for Pongo, he was delighted. He shook hands with Timmy's tail several times, and was disappointed that Timmy took no notice of him.

'Hallo! What's Barker gnawing at?' suddenly said Dick. 'Raw meat! How did it come here? Do you suppose the farmer has been by and given Timmy some? Well, why didn't he eat it, then?'

They all looked at Barker, who was gnawing some meat on the ground. Growler ran to it too. But Timmy would not go near it. Nor would Pongo. Timmy put his tail down and Pongo hid his furry face behind his paws.

'Funny,' said the children, puzzled at the queer behaviour of the two animals. Then suddenly they understood – for poor Barker suddenly gave a terrible whine, shivered from head to foot, and rolled over on his side.

'Jiminy – it's poisoned!' yelled Nobby, and kicked Growler away from the meat. He picked Barker up, and to the children's utter dismay they saw that Nobby was crying.

'He's done for,' said the boy, in a choking voice. 'Poor old Barker.'

Carrying Barker in his arms, with Growler and Pongo behind him, poor Nobby stumbled down the hill. No one liked to follow him. Poisoned meat! What a terrible thing.

Chapter Thirteen

JULIAN THINKS OF A PLAN

GEORGE was trembling. Her legs felt as if they wouldn't hold her up, and she sank down on the ledge. She put her arms round Timmy.

'Oh, Timmy! That meat was meant for you! Oh, thank goodness, thank goodness you were clever enough not to touch it! Timmy, you might have been poisoned!'

Timmy licked his mistress soberly. The others stood round, staring, not knowing what to think. Poor Barker! Would he die? Suppose it had been old Timmy? They had left him all alone, and he might have eaten the meat and died.

'I'll never, never leave you up here alone again!' said George.

'Who threw him the poisoned meat, do you think?' said Anne, in a small voice.

'Who do you suppose?' said George, in a hard, scornful voice. 'Lou and Tiger Dan!'

'They want to get us away from here, that's plain,' said Dick. 'But again – why?'

'What can there be about this place that makes the men want to get rid of us all?' wondered Julian. 'They're real rogues. Poor Nobby. He must have an awful life with them. And now they've gone and poisoned his dog.'

Nobody felt like eating very much that evening. Anne got out the bread and the butter and a pot of jam. George wouldn't eat anything. What a horrid end to a lovely day!

They all went to bed early, and nobody objected when Julian said he was going to lock both the caravans. 'Not that I think either Lou or Dan will be up here tonight,' he said. 'But you never know!'

Whether they came or not the children didn't know, for although Timmy began to bark loudly in the middle of the night, and scraped frantically at the shut door of George's caravan, there was nothing to be seen or heard when Julian opened his door and flashed on his torch.

Timmy didn't bark any more. He lay quite quietly sleeping with one ear cocked. Julian lay in bed and thought hard. Probably Lou and Dan had come creeping up in the dark, hoping that Timmy had taken the meat and been poisoned. But when they heard him bark, they knew he was all right, and they must have gone away again. What plan would they make next?

'There's something behind all this,' Julian thought, again and again. 'But what can it be? Why do they want us out of this particular spot?'

He couldn't imagine. He fell asleep at last with a vague plan in his mind. He would tell it to the others tomorrow. Perhaps if he could make Lou and Dan think they had all gone off for the day – with Timmy – but really, he, Julian, would be left behind, in hiding – maybe he could find out something, if Lou and Dan came along . . .

Julian fell asleep in the middle of thinking out his plan. Like the others, he dreamt of elephants squirting him with water, of Pongo chasing the monkeys, of the dogs playing football with excited yaps – and then into the dream came lumps of poisoned meat! Horrid.

Anne woke with a jump, having dreamt that someone had put poison into the hard-boiled eggs they were going to eat. She lay trembling in her bunk, and called to George in a small voice.

'George! I've been having an awful dream!'

George woke up, and Timmy stirred and stretched himself. George switched on her torch.

'I've been having beastly dreams, too,' she said. 'I dreamt that those men were after Timmy. I'll leave my torch on for a bit and we'll talk. I expect that with all the excitement we've had today, and the horrid end to it this evening, we're just in the mood for horrid dreams! Still – they are only dreams.'

'Woof,' said Timmy, and scratched himself.

'Don't,' said George. 'You shake the whole caravan when you do that, Timmy. Stop it.'

Timmy stopped. He sighed and lay down heavily. He put his head on his paws and looked sleepily at George, as if to say, 'put that torch out. I want to go to sleep.'

The next morning was not so warm, and the sky was cloudy. Nobody felt very cheerful, because they kept thinking of Nobby and poor Barker. They ate their breakfast almost in silence, and then Anne and George began to stack the plates, ready to take them to the spring to rinse.

'*I'll* go to the farm this morning,' said Julian. 'You sit on the ledge and take the field-glasses, Dick. We'll see if Nobby goes out in his boat and waves. I've an idea that he won't want us down in the camp this morning. If he suspects his Uncle Dan and Lou of putting down the meat that poisoned Barker, he'll probably have had a frightful row with them.'

He went off to the farm with two empty baskets. Mrs Mackie was ready for him, and he bought a further supply of delicious-looking food. Her present this time was a round ginger cake, warm from the oven!

'Do the circus folk come up here often to buy food?' asked Julian, as he paid Mrs Mackie.

'They come sometimes,' said Mrs Mackie. 'I don't mind the women or the children – dirty though they are, and not above taking one of my chickens now and again – but it's the men I can't abide. There were two here last year, messing about in the hills, that my husband had to send off quick.'

Julian pricked up his ears. 'Two men? What were they like?'

'Ugly fellows,' said Mrs Mackie. 'And one had the yellowest teeth I ever saw. Bad-tempered chaps, both of them. They came up here at night, and we were afraid our chickens would go. They swore they weren't after our chickens – but what else would they be up here at night for?'

'I can't imagine,' said Julian. He was sure that the two men Mrs Mackie spoke of were Lou and Tiger Dan. Why did they wander about in the hills at night?

He went off with the food. When he got near the camping-place, Dick called to him excitedly.

'Hey, Julian! Come and look through the glasses. Nobby's out in his boat with Pongo, and I simply can't make out what it is they're both waving.'

Julian took the glasses and looked through them. Far down the hill, on the surface of the lake, floated Nobby's little boat. In it was Nobby, and with him was Pongo. Both of them were waving something bright red.

'Can't see what they're waving – but that doesn't matter,' said Julian. 'The thing is – what they're waving is red, not white. Red for danger. He's warning us.'

'Golly – I didn't think of that. What an idiot I am!' said Dick. 'Yes – red for danger. What's up, I wonder?'

'Well, it's clear we'd better not go down to the camp today,' said Julian. 'And it's also clear that whatever danger there is, is pretty bad – because both he *and* Pongo are waving red cloths – doubly dangerous!'

'Julian, you're jolly sharp,' said George, who was listening. 'You're the only one of us who tumbled to all that. Double-danger. What can it be?'

'Perhaps it means danger down at the camp, and danger here too,' said Julian, thoughtfully. 'I hope poor old Nobby is all right. Tiger Dan is so jolly beastly to him. I bet he's had a beating or two since last night.'

'It's a shame!' said Dick.

'Don't tell Anne we think there is double-danger about,' said Julian, seeing Anne coming back from the spring. 'She'll be scared. She was hoping we wouldn't have an adventure these hols – and now we seem to be plunged into the middle of one. Golly I really think we ought to leave these hills and go on somewhere else.'

But he only said this half-heartedly, because he was burning to solve the curious mystery behind Lou's behaviour and Dan's. The others pounced on him at once.

'We can't leave! Don't be a coward, Ju!'

'I *won't* leave. Nor will Timmy.'

'Shut up,' said Julian. 'Here comes Anne.'

They said no more. Julian watched Nobby for a little while longer. Then the boy and the chimpanzee drew in to the shore and disappeared.

When they were all sitting together on the ledge,

Julian proposed the plan he had been thinking out the night before.

'I'd like to find out what there is about this place that attracts Lou and Dan,' he said. 'There is *something* not far from here that makes the men want to get rid of us. Now suppose we four and Timmy go off down the hill and pass the camp, and yell out to Nobby that we're *all* – *all* of us – going to the town for the day – and you three do go, but I slip back up the hill – maybe Lou and Dan will come up here, and if I'm in hiding I shall see what they're up to!'

'You mean, we'll all four pretend to go to town – but really only three of us go, and you get back and hide,' said Dick. 'I see. It's a good idea.'

'And you'll hide somewhere and watch for the men to come,' said George. 'Well, for goodness sake don't let them see you, Julian. You won't have Timmy, you know! Those men could make mincemeat of you if they wanted to.'

'Oh, they'd want to all right. I know that,' said Julian grimly. 'But you can be sure I'll be jolly well hidden.'

'I don't see why we can't have a good look round and see if we can't find the cave or whatever it is the men want to come to,' said Dick. 'If they can find it, we can, too!'

'We don't know that it *is* a cave,' said Julian. 'We haven't any idea at all what attracts the men up here. Mrs Mackie said they were up here last year, too, and the farmer had to drive them away. They thought the men were after the chickens – but I don't think so. There's *some*thing in these hills that makes the men want to get us away.'

'Let's have a good look round,' said George, feeling suddenly thrilled. 'I've gone all adventurous again!'

'Oh dear!' said Anne. But she couldn't help feeling rather thrilled, too. They all got up and Timmy followed, wagging his tail. He was pleased that his friends hadn't gone off and left him on guard by himself that morning.

'We'll all go different ways,' said Julian. 'Up, down and sideways. I'll go up.'

They separated and went off, George and Timmy together, of course. They hunted in the hillside for possible caves, or even for some kind of hiding-place. Timmy put his head down every rabbit-hole and felt very busy indeed.

After about half an hour the others heard Julian yelling. They ran back to the caravans, sure that he had found something exciting.

But he hadn't. He had simply got tired of hunting and decided to give it up. He shook his head when they rushed up to him, shouting to know what he had found.

'Nothing,' he said. 'I'm fed up with looking. There's not a cave anywhere here. I'm sure of that! Anyone else found anything?'

'Not a thing,' said everyone in disappointment. 'What shall we do now?'

'Put our plan into action,' said Julian, promptly. 'Let the men themselves show us what they're after. Off we go down the hills, and we'll yell out to Nobby that we're off for the day – and we'll hope that Lou and Tiger Dan will hear us!'

Chapter Fourteen

A VERY GOOD HIDING-PLACE

THEY went down the hill with Timmy. Julian gave Dick some instructions. 'Have a meal in the town,' he said. 'Keep away for the day, so as to give the men a chance to come up the hill. Go to the post office and see if there are any letters for us – and buy some tins of fruit. They'll make a nice change.'

'Right, Captain!' said Dick. 'And just you be careful, old boy. These men will stick at nothing – bad-tempered brutes they are.'

'Look after the girls,' said Julian. 'Don't let George do anything mad!'

Dick grinned. 'Who can stop George doing what she wants to? Not me!'

They were now at the bottom of the hill. The circus camp lay nearby. The children could hear the barking of the dogs and the shrill trumpeting of Old Lady.

They looked about for Nobby. He was nowhere to be seen. Blow! It wouldn't be any good setting off to the town and laying such a good plan if they couldn't tell Nobby they were going!

Nobody dared to go into the camp. Julian thought of the two red cloths that Nobby and Pongo had waved. Double-danger! It would be wise not to go into the camp that morning. He stood still, undecided what to do.

Then he opened his mouth and yelled:

'Nobby! NOBBY!'

No answer and no Nobby. The elephant man heard him shouting and came up. 'Do you want Nobby? I'll fetch him.'

'Thanks,' said Julian.

The little man went off, whistling. Soon Nobby appeared from behind a caravan, looking rather scared. He didn't come near Julian, but stood a good way away, looking pale and troubled.

'Nobby! We're going into the town for the day,' yelled Julian at the top of his voice. 'We're . . .'

Tiger Dan suddenly appeared behind Nobby and grabbed his arm fiercely. Nobby put up a hand to protect his face, as if he expected a blow. Julian yelled again:

'We're going into the town, Nobby! We shan't be back till evening. Can you hear me? WE'RE GOING TO THE TOWN!'

The whole camp must have heard Julian. But he was quite determined that, whoever else didn't hear, Tiger Dan certainly should.

Nobby tried to shake off his uncle's hand, and opened his mouth to yell back something. But Dan roughly put his hand across Nobby's mouth and hauled him away, shaking him as a dog shakes a rat.

'HOW'S BARKER?' yelled Julian. But Nobby had disappeared, dragged into his uncle's caravan by Dan. The little elephant man heard, however.

'Barker's bad,' he said. 'Not dead yet. But nearly. Never saw a dog so sick in my life. Nobby's fair upset!'

The children walked off with Timmy. George had had to hold his collar all the time, for once he saw Dan he growled without stopping, and tried to get away from George.

'Thank goodness Barker isn't dead,' said Anne. 'I do hope he'll get better.'

'Not much chance,' said Julian. 'That meat must have been chockful of poison. Poor old Nobby. How awful to be under the thumb of a fellow like Tiger Dan.'

'I just simply can't *imagine* him as a clown – Tiger Dan, I mean,' said Anne. 'Clowns are always so merry and gay and jolly.'

'Well, that's just acting,' said Dick. 'A clown needn't be the same out of the ring as he has to be when he's in it. If you look at photographs of clowns when they're just being ordinary men, they've got quite sad faces.'

'Well, Tiger Dan hasn't got a sad face. He's got a nasty, ugly, savage, cruel, fierce one,' said Anne, looking quite fierce herself.

That made the others laugh. Dick turned round to see if anyone was watching them walking towards the bus-stop, where the buses turned to go to the town.

'Lou the acrobat is watching us,' he said. 'Good! Can he see the bus-stop from where he is, Ju?'

Julian turned round. 'Yes, he can. He'll watch to see us all get into the bus – so I'd better climb in, too, and I'll get out at the first stop, double back, and get into the hills by some path he won't be able to see.'

'Right,' said Dick, enjoying the thought of playing a trick on Lou. 'Come on. There's the bus. We'll have to run for it.'

They all got into the bus. Lou was still watching, a small figure very far away. Dick felt inclined to wave cheekily to him, but didn't.

The bus set off. They took three tickets for the town and one for the nearest stop. Timmy had a ticket, too, which he wore proudly in his collar. He loved going in a bus.

Julian got out at the first stop. 'Well, see you this evening!' he said. 'Send Timmy on ahead to the caravans when you come back – just in case the men are anywhere about. I may not be able to warn you.'

'Right,' said Dick. 'Good-bye – and good luck!'

Julian waved and set off back down the road he had come. He saw a little lane leading off up into the hills and decided to take it. It led him not very far from Mrs Mackie's farm, so he soon knew where he was. He went back to the caravans, and quickly made himself some sandwiches and cut some cake to take to his hiding-place. He might have a long wait!

'Now – where shall I hide?' thought the boy. 'I want somewhere that will give me a view of the track so that I can see when the men come up it. And yet it must be somewhere that gives me a good view of their doings, too. What would be the best place?'

A tree? No, there wasn't one that was near enough or thick enough. Behind a bush? No, the men might easily come round it and see him. What about the middle of a thick gorse bush? That might be a good idea.

But Julian gave that up very quickly, for he found the bush far too prickly to force his way into the middle. He scratched his arms and legs terribly.

'Blow!' he said. 'I really must make up my mind, or the men may be here before I'm in hiding!'

And then he suddenly had a real brainwave, and he crowed in delight. Of course! The very place!

'I'll climb up on to the roof of one of the caravans!' thought Julian. 'Nobody will see me there – and certainly nobody would guess I was there! That really is a fine idea. I shall have a fine view of the track and a first-rate view of the men and where they go!'

It wasn't very easy to climb up on to the high roof. He had to get a rope, loop it at the end, and try to lasso the chimney in order to climb up.

He managed to lasso the chimney, and the rope hung down over the side of the caravan, ready for him to swarm up. He threw his packet of food up on to the roof and then climbed up himself. He pulled up the rope and coiled it beside him.

Then he lay down flat. He was certain that nobody could see him from below. Of course, if the men went higher up the hill and looked down on the caravans, he could easily be spotted – but he would have to chance that.

He lay there quite still, watching the lake, and keeping eyes and ears open for anyone coming up the hillside. He was glad that it was not a very hot sunny day, or he would have been cooked up on the roof. He wished he had thought of filling a bottle with water in case he was thirsty.

He saw spires of smoke rising from where the circus camp lay, far below. He saw a couple of boats on the lake, a good way round the water – people fishing, he supposed. He watched a couple of rabbits come out and play on the hillside just below.

The sun came out from behind the clouds for about ten minutes and Julian began to feel uncomfortably hot. Then it went in again and he felt better.

He suddenly heard somebody whistling and stiffened himself in expectation – but it was only someone belong-

ing to the farm, going down the hill some distance away.
The whistle had carried clearly in the still air.

Then he got bored. The rabbits went in, and not even
a butterfly sailed by. He could see no birds except a
yellow-hammer that sat on the topmost spray of a bush
and sang: 'Little-bit-of-bread-and-no-cheese', over and
over again in a most maddening manner.

Then it gave a cry of alarm and flew off. It had heard
something that frightened it.

Julian heard something, too, and glued his eyes to the
track that led up the hill. His heart began to beat. He
could see two men. Were they Lou and Dan?

He did not dare to raise his head to see them when they
came nearer in case they spotted him. But he knew their
voices when they came near enough!

Yes – it was Lou and Tiger Dan all right. There was
no mistaking those two harsh, coarse voices. The men
came right into the hollow, and Julian heard them
talking.

'Yes, there's nobody here. Those kids have really gone
off for the day at least – and taken that wretched dog
with them!'

'I saw them get on the bus, dog and all, I told you,'
growled Lou. 'There'll be nobody here for the day. We
can get what we want to.'

'Let's go and get it, then,' said Dan.

Julian waited to see where they would go to. But they
didn't go out of the hollow. They stayed there, apparently
beside the caravans. Julian did not dare to look over the
edge of the roof to see what they were up to. He was glad
he had fastened all the windows and locked the doors.

Then there began some curious scuffling sounds, and

the men panted. The caravan on which Julian was lying began to shake a little.

'What *are* they doing?' thought Julian in bewilderment. In intense curiosity he slid quietly to the edge of the caravan roof and cautiously peeped over, though he had firmly made up his mind not to do this on any account.

He looked down on the ground. There was nobody there at all. Perhaps the men were the other side. He slid carefully across and peeped over the opposite side of the caravan, which was still shaking a little, as if the men were bumping against it.

There was nobody the other side either! How very extraordinary! 'Golly! They must be underneath the caravan!' thought Julian, going back to the middle of the roof. 'Underneath! What in the wide world for?'

It was quite impossible to see underneath the caravan from where he was, so he had to lie quietly and wonder about the men's doings. They grunted and groaned, and seemed to be scraping and scrabbling about, but nothing happened. Then Julian heard them scrambling out from underneath, angry and disappointed.

'Give us a cigarette,' said Lou in a disagreeable voice. 'I'm fed up with this. Have to shift this van. Those tiresome brats! What did they want to choose this spot for?'

Julian heard a match struck and smelt cigarette smoke. Then he got a shock. The caravan he was on began to move! Heavens! Were the men going to push it over the ledge and send it rolling down the hillside?

Chapter Fifteen

SEVERAL THINGS HAPPEN

JULIAN was suddenly very scared. He wondered if he had
better slide off the roof and run. He wouldn't have much
chance if the caravan went hurtling down the hill! But
he didn't move. He clung to the chimney with both
hands, whilst the men shoved hard against the caravan.

It ran a few feet to the rocky ledge, and then stopped.
Julian felt his forehead getting very damp, and he saw
that his hands were trembling. He felt ashamed of being
so scared, but he couldn't help it.

'Hey! Don't send it down the hill!' said Lou in alarm,
and Julian's heart felt lighter. So they didn't mean to
destroy the caravan in that way! They had just moved it
to get at something underneath. But what could it be?
Julian racked his brains to try and think what the floor
of the hollow had been like when Dobby and Trotter
pulled their caravans into it. As far as he could remember
it was just an ordinary heathery hollow.

The men were now scrabbling away again by the back
steps of the caravan. Julian was absolutely eaten up with
curiosity, but he did not dare even to move. He could
find out the secret when the men had gone. Meantime he
really must be patient or he would spoil everything.

There was some muttered talking, but Julian couldn't
catch a word. Then, quite suddenly, there was complete
and utter silence. Not a word. Not a bump against the
caravan. Not a pant or even a grunt. Nothing at all.

Julian lay still. Maybe the men were still there. He wasn't going to give himself away. He lay for quite a long time, waiting and wondering. But he heard nothing.

Then he saw a robin fly to a nearby bramble spray. It flicked its wings and looked about for crumbs. It was a robin that came around when the children were having a meal – but it was not as tame as most robins, and would not fly down until the children had left the hollow.

Then a rabbit popped out of a hole on the hillside and capered about, running suddenly up to the hollow.

'Well,' thought Julian, 'it's plain the men aren't here now, or the birds and animals wouldn't be about like this. There's another rabbit. Those men have gone somewhere – though goodness knows where. I can peep over now and have a look, quite safely, I should think.'

He slid himself round and peered over the roof at the back end of the caravan. He looked down at the ground. There was absolutely nothing to be seen to tell him what the men had been doing, or where they had gone! The heather grew luxuriantly there as it did everywhere else. There was nothing to show what the men had been making such a disturbance about.

'This is really very queer,' thought Julian, beginning to wonder if he had been dreaming. 'The men are certainly gone – vanished into thin air, apparently! Dare I get down and explore a bit? No, I daren't. The men may appear at any moment, and it's quite on the cards they'll lose their temper if they find me here, and chuck both me and the caravans down the hill! It's pretty steep just here, too.'

He lay there, thinking. He suddenly felt very hungry and thirsty. Thank goodness he had been sensible enough

to take food up to the roof! He could at least have a meal
while he was waiting for the men to come back – if they
ever did!

He began to eat his sandwiches. They tasted very good
indeed. He finished them all and began on the cake.
That was good, too. He had brought a few plums up as
well, and was very glad of them because he was thirsty.
He flicked the plum stones from the roof before he
thought what he was doing.

'Dash! Why did I do that? If the men notice them
they may remember they weren't there before. Still,
they've most of them gone into the heather!'

The sun came out a little and Julian felt hot. He
wished the men would come again and go down the hill.
He was tired of lying flat on the hard roof. Also he was
terribly sleepy. He yawned silently and shut his
eyes.

How long he slept he had no idea – but he was suddenly awakened by feeling the caravan being moved
again! He clutched the chimney in alarm, listening to
the low voices of the two men.

They were pulling the caravan back into place again.
Soon it was in the same position as before. Then Julian
heard a match struck and smelt smoke again.

The men went and sat on the rocky ledge and took
out food they had brought. Julian did not dare to peep at
them, though he felt sure they had their backs to him.
The men ate, and talked in low voices, and then, to
Julian's dismay, they lay down and went to sleep! He
knew that they were asleep because he could hear them
snoring.

'Am I going to stay on this awful roof all day long?' he

thought. 'I'm getting so cramped, lying flat like this. I want to sit up!'

'R-r-r-r-r-r!' snored Lou and Dan. Julian felt that surely it would be all right to sit up now that the men were obviously asleep. So he sat up cautiously, stretching himself with pleasure.

He looked down on the two men, who were lying on their backs with their mouths open. Beside them were two neat sacks, strong and thick. Julian wondered what was inside them. They certainly had not had them when they came up the track.

The boy gazed down the hillside, frowning, trying to probe the mystery of where the men had been, and what they were doing up here – and suddenly he jumped violently. He stared as if he could not believe his eyes.

A squat and ugly face was peering out from a bramble bush there. There was almost no nose, and an enormous mouth. Who could it be? Was it someone spying on Lou and Dan? But what a face! It didn't seem human.

A hand came up to rub the face – and Julian saw that it was hairy. With a start he knew who the face belonged to – Pongo the chimpanzee! No wonder he had thought it such an ugly, inhuman face. It was all right on a chimp, of course – quite a nice face – but not on a man.

Pongo stared at Julian solemnly, and Julian stared back, his mind in a whirl. What was Pongo doing there? Was Nobby with him? If so, Nobby was in danger, for at any moment the men might wake up. He couldn't think what to do. If he called out to warn Nobby, he would wake the men.

Pongo was pleased to see Julian, and did not seem to think the roof of a caravan a curious place to be in at all.

After all, *he* often went up on the roofs of caravans. He nodded and blinked at the boy, and then scratched his head for a long time.

Then beside him appeared Nobby's face – a tear-stained face, bruised and swollen. He suddenly saw Julian looking over the roof of the caravan, and his mouth fell open in surprise. He seemed about to call out, and Julian shook his head frantically to stop him, pointing downwards to try and warn Nobby that somebody was there.

But Nobby didn't understand. He grinned and, to Julian's horror, began to climb up the hillside to the rocky ledge! The men were sleeping there, and Julian saw with dismay that Nobby would probably heave himself up right on top of them.

'Look out!' he said, in a low, urgent voice. 'Look out, you fathead!'

But it was too late. Nobby heaved himself up on to the ledge, and, to his utmost horror, found himself sprawling on top of Tiger Dan! He gave a yell and tried to slide away – but Dan, rousing suddenly, shot out a hand and gripped him.

Lou woke up, too. The men glared at poor Nobby, and the boy began to tremble, and to beg for mercy.

'I didn't know you were here, I swear it! Let me go, let me go! I only came up to look for my knife that I lost yesterday!'

Dan shook him savagely. 'How long have you been here? You been spying?'

'No, no! I've only just come! I've been at the camp all morning – you ask Larry and Rossy. I been helping them!'

'You been spying on us, that's what you've been doing!' said Lou, in a cold, hard voice that filled the listening Julian with dread. 'You've had plenty of beatings this week, but seemingly they ain't enough. Well, up here, there's nobody to hear your yells, see? So we'll show you what a real beating is! And if you can walk down to the camp after it, I'll be surprised.'

Nobby was terrified. He begged for mercy, he promised to do anything the men asked him, and tried to jerk his poor swollen face away from Dan's hard hands.

Julian couldn't bear it. He didn't want to give away the fact that it was he who had been spying, nor did he want to fight the men at all, for he was pretty certain he would get the worst of it. But nobody could lie in silence, watching two men treat a young boy in such a way. He made up his mind to leap off the roof right on to the men, and to rescue poor Nobby if he could.

Nobby gave an anguished yell as Lou gave him a flick with his leather belt – but before Julian could jump down to help him, somebody else bounded up! Somebody who bared his teeth and made ugly animal noises of rage, somebody whose arms were far stronger than either Lou's or Dan's – somebody who loved poor Nobby, and wasn't going to let him be beaten any more!

It was Pongo. The chimpanzee had been watching the scene with his sharp little eyes. He had still hidden himself in the bush, for he was afraid of Lou and Dan – but now, hearing Nobby's cries, he leapt out of the brambles and flung himself on the astonished men.

He bit Lou's arm hard. Then he bit Dan's leg. The men yelled loudly, much more loudly than poor Nobby had. Lou lashed out with his leather belt, and it caught

Pongo on the shoulder. The chimpanzee made a shrill chattering noise, and leapt on Lou with his arms open, clasping the man to him, trying to bite his throat.

Tiger Dan rushed down the hill at top speed, terrified of the angry chimpanzee. Lou yelled to Nobby.

'Call him off! He'll kill me!'

'Pongo!' shouted Nobby. 'Stop it! Pongo! Come here.'

Pongo gave Nobby a look of the greatest surprise. 'What!' he seemed to say, 'you won't let me punish this bad man who beat you? Well, well – whatever you say must be right!'

And the chimpanzee, giving Lou one last vicious nip, let the man go. Lou followed Dan down the hill at top speed, and Julian heard him crashing through the bushes as if a hundred chimpanzees were after him.

Nobby sat down, trembling. Pongo, not quite sure if his beloved friend was angry with him or not, crept up to him putting a paw on the boy's knee. Nobby put his arm round the anxious animal, and Pongo chattered with joy.

Julian slid down from the roof of the caravan and went to Nobby. He, too, sat down beside him. He put his arm round the trembling boy and gave him a hug.

'I was just coming to give you a hand, when Pongo shot up the hill,' he said.

'Were you really?' said Nobby, his face lighting up. 'You're a real friend, you are. Good as Pongo, here.'

And Julian felt quite proud to be ranked in bravery with the chimpanzee!

Chapter Sixteen

A SURPRISING DISCOVERY

'LISTEN – somebody's coming!' said Nobby, and Pongo gave an ugly growl. The sound of voices could be heard coming up the hill. Then a dog barked.

'It's all right. It's Timmy – and the others,' said Julian, unspeakably glad to welcome them back. He stood up and yelled.

'All right! Come along!'

George, Timmy, Dick and Anne came running up the track. 'Hallo!' shouted Dick. 'We thought it would be safe, because we saw Lou and Dan in the distance, running along at the bottom of the hill. I say – there's Pongo!'

Pongo shook hands with Dick, and then went to the back of Timmy, to shake hands with his tail. But Timmy was ready for him, and backing round, he held out his paw to Pongo instead. It was very funny to see the two animals solemnly shaking hands with one another.

'Hallo, Nobby!' said Dick. 'Goodness – what have you been doing to yourself? You look as if you've been in the wars.'

'Well, I have, rather,' said Nobby, with a feeble grin. He was very much shaken, and did not get up. Pongo ran to Anne and tried to put his arms round her.

'Oh, Pongo – you squeeze too hard,' said Anne. 'Julian, did anything happen? Did the men come? Have you any news?'

'Plenty,' said Julian. 'But what I want first is a jolly good drink. I've had none all day. Ginger-beer, I think.'

'We're all thirsty. I'll get five bottles – no, six, because I expect Pongo would like some.'

Pongo loved ginger-beer. He sat down with the children on the rocky ledge, and took his glass from Anne just like a child. Timmy was a little jealous, but as he didn't like ginger-beer he couldn't make a fuss.

Julian began to tell the others about his day, and how he had hidden on the caravan roof. He described how the men had come – and had gone under the caravan – and then moved it. They all listened with wide eyes. What a story!

Then Nobby told his part. 'I butted in and almost gave the game away,' he said, when Julian had got as far as the men falling asleep and snoring. 'But, you see, I had to come and warn you. Lou and Dan swear they'll poison Timmy somehow, even if they have to dope him, put him into a sack and take him down to the camp to do it. Or they might knock him on the head.'

'Let them try!' said George, in her fiercest voice, and put her arm round Timmy. Pongo at once put his arm round Timmy too.

'And they said they'd damage your caravans too – maybe put a fire underneath and burn them up,' went on Nobby.

The four children stared at him in horror. 'But they wouldn't do a thing like that, surely?' said Julian, at last. 'They'd get into trouble with the police if they did.'

'Well, I'm just telling you what they said,' Nobby went on. 'You don't know Lou and Tiger Dan like I do. They'll stick at nothing to get their way – or to get anybody *out* of their way. They tried to poison Timmy, didn't they? And poor old Barker got it instead.'

'Is – is Barker – all right?' asked Anne.

'No,' said Nobby. 'He's dying, I think. I've given him to Lucilla to dose. She's a marvel with sick animals. I've put Growler with the other dogs. He's safe with them.'

He stared round at the other children, his mouth trembling, sniffing as if he had a bad cold.

'I dursent go back,' he said, in a low voice, 'I dursent. They'll half-kill me.'

'You're not going back, so that's settled,' said Julian, in a brisk voice. 'You're staying here with us. We shall love to have you. It was jolly decent of you to come up and warn us – and bad luck to have got caught like that. You're our friend now – and we'll stick together.'

Nobby couldn't say a word, but his face shone. He rubbed a dirty hand across his eyes, then grinned his old grin. He nodded his head, not trusting himself to speak, and the children all thought how nice he was. Poor old Nobby.

They finished their ginger-beer and then Julian got up. 'And now,' he said, 'we will do a little exploring and find out where those men went, shall we?'

'Oh yes!' cried George, who had sat still quite long enough. 'We *must* find out! Do we have to get under the caravan, Julian?'

' 'Fraid so,' said Julian. 'You sit there quietly, Nobby, and keep guard in case Lou or Dan come back.'

He didn't think for a moment that they would, but he could see that Nobby needed to sit quietly for a while. Nobby, however, had different ideas. He was going to share this adventure!

'Timmy's guard enough, and so is Pongo,' he said 'They'll hear anyone coming half a mile away. I'm in on this!'

And he was. He went scrabbling underneath the low-swung base of the caravan with the others, eager to find out anything he could.

But it was impossible to explore down in the heather, with the caravan base just over their heads. They had no room at all. Like Dan and Lou they soon felt that they would have to move the van.

It took all five of them, with Pongo giving a shove, too, to move the caravan a few feet away. Then down they dropped to the thick carpet of heather again.

The tufts came up easily by the roots, because the men had already pulled them up once that day and then re-planted them. The children dragged up a patch of heather about five feet square, and then gave an exclamation.

'Look! Boards under the heather!'

'Laid neatly across and across. What for?'

'Pull them up!'

The boys pulled up the planks one by one and piled them on one side. Then they saw that the boards had closed up the entrance of a deep hole. 'I'll get my torch,' said Julian. He fetched it and flashed it on.

The light showed them a dark hole, going down into the hillside, with footholds sticking out of one side. They all sat and gazed down in excitement.

'To think we went and put our caravan *exactly* over the entrance of the men's hiding-place!' said Dick. 'No wonder they were wild! No wonder they changed their minds and told us we could go down to the lake and camp there instead of here!'

'Gosh!' said Julian, staring into the hole. 'So that's where the men went! Where does it lead to? They were down there a mighty long time. They were clever enough to replace the planks and drag some of the heather over them, too, to hide them when they went down.'

Pongo suddenly took it into his head to go down the hole. Down he went, feeling for the footholds with his hairy feet, grinning up at the others. He disappeared at the bottom. Julian's torch could not pick him out at all.

'Hey, Pongo! Don't lose yourself down there!' called Nobby, anxiously. But Pongo had gone.

'Blow him!' said Nobby. 'He'll never find his way back,

if he goes wandering about underground. I'll have to go after him. Can I have your torch, Julian?'

'I'll come too,' said Julian. 'George, get me your torch as well, will you?'

'It's broken,' said George. 'I dropped it last night. And nobody else has got one.'

'What an awful nuisance!' said Julian. 'I want us to go and explore down there – but we can't with only one torch. Well, I'll just go down with Nobby and get Pongo – have a quick look round and come back. I may see something worth seeing!'

Nobby went down first, and Julian followed, the others all kneeling round the hole, watching them enviously. They disappeared.

'Pongo!' yelled Nobby. 'Pongo! Come here, you idiot!'

Pongo had not gone very far. He didn't like the dark down there very much, and he came to Nobby as soon as he saw the light of the torch. The boys found themselves in a narrow passage at the bottom of the hole, which widened as they went further into the hill.

'Must be caves somewhere,' said Julian, flashing his torch round. 'We know that a lot of springs run out of this hill. I daresay that through the centuries the water has eaten away the softer stuff and made caves and tunnels everywhere in the hill. And somewhere in a cave Lou and Dan store away things they don't want anyone to know about. Stolen goods, probably.'

The passage ended in a small cave that seemed to have no other opening out of it at all. There was nothing in it. Julian flashed his torch up and down the walls.

He saw footholds up one part, and traced them to a hole in the roof, which must have been made, years before, by running water. 'That's the way we go!' he said. 'Come on.'

'Wait!' said Nobby. 'Isn't your torch getting rather faint?'

'Goodness – yes!' said Julian in alarm, and shook his torch violently to make the light brighter. But the battery had almost worn out, and no better light came. Instead the light grew even fainter, until it was just a pin-prick in the torch.

'Come on – we'd better get back at once,' said Julian, feeling a bit scared. 'I don't want to wander about here in the pitch dark. Not my idea of fun at all.'

Nobby took firm hold of Pongo's hairy paw and equally firm hold of Julian's jersey. He didn't mean to lose either of them! The light in the torch went out completely. Now they must find their way back in black darkness.

Julian felt round for the beginning of the passage that led back to the hole. He found it and made his way up it, feeling the sides with his hands. It wasn't a pleasant experience at all, and Julian was thankful that he and Nobby had only gone a little way into the hill. It would have been like a nightmare if they had gone well in, and then found themselves unable to see the way back.

They saw a faint light shining further on and guessed it was the daylight shining down the entrance-hole. They stumbled thankfully towards it. They looked up and saw the anxious faces of the other three peering down at them, unable to see them.

'We're back!' called Julian, beginning to climb up. 'My torch went out, and we daren't go very far. We've got Pongo, though.'

The others helped to pull them out at the top of the hole. Julian told them about the hole in the roof of the little cave.

'That's were the men went,' he said. 'And tomorrow, when we've all bought torches, and matches and candles, that's where we're going, too! We'll go down to the town and buy what we want, and come back and do a Really Good Exploration!'

'We're going to have an adventure after all,' said Anne, in rather a small voice.

' 'Fraid so,' said Julian. 'But you can stay at the farm with Mrs Mackie for the day, Anne dear. Don't you come with us.'

'If you're going on an adventure, I'm coming, too,' said Anne. 'So there! I wouldn't *dream* of not coming.'

'All right,' said Julian. 'We'll all go together. Golly, things are getting exciting!'

Chapter Seventeen

ANOTHER VISIT FROM LOU AND DAN

NOBODY disturbed the children that night, and Timmy did not bark once. Nobby slept on a pile of rugs in the boy's caravan, and Pongo cuddled up to him. The chimpanzee seemed delighted at staying with the caravanners. Timmy was rather jealous that another animal should be with them, and wouldn't take any notice of Pongo at all.

The next morning, after breakfast, the children discussed who was to go down to the town. 'Not Nobby and Pongo, because they wouldn't be allowed in the bus together,' said Julian. 'They had better stay behind.'

'Not by ourselves?' said Nobby, looking alarmed. 'Suppose Lou and Uncle Dan come up? Even if I've got Pongo I'd be scared.'

'Well, I'll stay here, too,' said Dick. 'We don't all need to go to buy torches. Don't forget to post that letter to Daddy and Mother, Julian.'

They had written a long letter to their parents, telling them of the exciting happenings. Julian put it into his pocket. 'I'll post it all right,' he said. 'Well, I suppose we might as well go now. Come on, girls. Keep a look-out, Dick, in case those rogues come back.'

George, Timmy, Anne and Julian went down the hill together, Timmy running on in front, his tail wagging nineteen to the dozen. Pongo climbed up to the roof of the red caravan to watch them go. Nobby and Dick sat

down in the warm sun on the ledge, their heads resting
on springy clumps of heather.

'It's nice up here,' said Nobby. 'Much nicer than down
below. I wonder what everyone is thinking about Pongo
and me. I bet Mr Gorgio, the head of the circus, is wild
that the chimpanzee's gone. I bet he'll send up to fetch
us.'

Nobby was right. Two people were sent up to get him –
Lou and Tiger Dan. They came creeping up through
the bracken and heather, keeping a sharp eye for Timmy
or Pongo.

Pongo sensed them long before they could be seen and
warned Nobby. Nobby went very pale. He was terrified
of the two scoundrels.

'Get into one of the caravans,' said Dick in a low voice.
'Go on. I'll deal with those fellows – if it *is* them. Pongo
will help me if necessary.'

Nobby scuttled into the green caravan and shut the
door. Dick sat where he was. Pongo squatted on the
roof of the caravan, watching.

Lou and Dan suddenly appeared. They saw Dick,
but did not see Pongo. They looked all round for the
others.

'What do you want?' said Dick.

'Nobby and Pongo,' said Lou with a scowl. 'Where are
they?'

'They're going to stay on with us,' said Dick.

'Oh, no, they're not!' said Tiger Dan. 'Nobby's in my
charge, see? I'm his uncle.'

'Funny sort of uncle,' remarked Dick. 'How's that dog
you poisoned, by the way?'

Tiger Dan went purple in the face. He looked as if he

would willingly have thrown Dick down the hill.

'You be careful what you say to me!' he said, beginning to shout.

Nobby, hidden in the caravan, trembled when he heard his uncle's angry yell. Pongo kept quite still, his face set and ugly.

'Well, you may as well say good-bye and go,' said Dick in a calm voice to Dan. 'I've told you that Nobby and Pongo are staying with us for the present.'

'Where *is* Nobby?' demanded Tiger Dan, looking as if he would burst with rage at any moment. 'Wait till I get my hands on him. Wait . . .'

He began to walk towards the caravans – but Pongo was not having any of that! He leapt straight off the roof on to the horrified man, and flung him to the ground. He made such a terrible snarling noise that Dan was terrified.

'Call him off!' he yelled. 'Lou, come and help.'

'Pongo won't obey *me*,' said Dick still sitting down looking quite undisturbed. 'You'd better go before he bites big pieces out of you.'

Dan staggered to the rock ledge, looking as if he would box Dick's ears. But the boy did not move, and somehow Dan did not dare to touch him. Pongo let him go and stood glowering at him, his great hairy arms hanging down his sides, ready to fly at either of the men if they came near.

Tiger Dan picked up a stone – and as quick as lightning Pongo flung himself on him again and sent the man rolling down the hill. Lou fled in terror. Dan got up and fled, too, yelling furiously as he went. Pongo chased them in delight. He, too, picked up stones and flung them

with a very accurate aim, so that Dick kept hearing yells of pain.

Pongo came back, looking extremely pleased with himself. He went to the green caravan, as Dick shouted to Nobby.

'All right, Nobby. They've gone. Pongo and I won the battle!'

Nobby came out. Pongo put his arm round him at once and chattered nonsense in his ear. Nobby looked rather ashamed of himself.

'Bit of a coward, aren't I?' he said. 'Leaving you out here all alone.'

'I enjoyed it,' said Dick truthfully. 'And I'm sure Pongo did!'

'You don't know what dangerous fellows Lou and Dan are,' said Nobby, looking down the hillside to make sure the men were really gone. 'I tell you they'd stick at nothing. They'd burn your caravans, hurl them down the hill, poison your dog, and do what harm they could to you, too. You don't know them like I do!'

'Well, as a matter of fact, we've had some pretty exciting adventures with men just as tough as Dan and Lou,' said Dick. 'We always seem to be falling into the middle of some adventure or other. Now, last hols we went to a place called Smuggler's Top – and, my word, the adventures we had there! You wouldn't believe them!'

'You tell me and Pongo,' said Nobby, sitting down beside Dick. 'We've plenty of time before the others come back.'

So Dick began to tell the tale of all the other thrilling adventures that the five of them had had, and the time flew. Both boys were surprised when they heard Timmy barking down the track, and knew that the others were back.

George came tearing up with Timmy at her heels. 'Are you all right? Did anything happen while we were away? Do you know, we saw Lou and Tiger Dan getting on the bus when we got off it! They were carrying bags as if they meant to go away and stay somewhere.'

Nobby brightened up at once. 'Did you really? Good! They came up here, you know, and Pongo chased them down the hill. They must have gone back to the camp, collected their bags, and gone to catch the bus. Hurrah!'

'We've got fine torches,' said Julian, and showed Dick his. 'Powerful ones. Here's one for you, Dick – and one for you, Nobby.'

'Oooh – thanks,' said Nobby. Then he went red. 'I haven't got enough money to pay you for such a grand torch,' he said awkwardly.

'It's a present for you,' said Anne at once, 'a present for a friend of ours, Nobby!'

'Coo! Thanks awfully,' said Nobby, looking quite overcome. 'I've never had a present before. You're decent kids, you are.'

Pongo held out his hand to Anne and made a chattering noise as if to say: 'What about one for me, too?'

'Oh – we didn't bring one for Pongo!' said Anne. 'Why ever didn't we?'

'Good thing you didn't,' said Nobby. 'He would have put it on and off all day long and wasted the battery in no time!'

'I'll give him my old torch,' said George. 'It's broken, but he won't mind that!'

Pongo was delighted with it. He kept pressing down
the knob that should make the light flash – and when
there was no light he looked all about on the ground as if
the light must have dropped out! The children roared at
him. He liked them to laugh at him. He did a little dance
all round them to show how pleased he was.

'Look here – wouldn't it be a jolly good time to explore
underground now that we know Lou and Dan are safely
out of the way?' asked Julian suddenly. 'If they've got
bags with them, surely that means they're going to spend
the night somewhere and won't be back till tomorrow at
least. We'd be quite safe to go down and explore.'

'Yes, we would,' said George eagerly. 'I'm longing to
get down there and Make Discoveries!'

'Well, let's have something to eat first,' said Dick. 'It's long past our dinner-time. It must be about half-past one. Yes, it is!'

'George and I will get you a meal,' said Anne. 'We called at the farm on our way up and got a lovely lot of food. Come on, George.'

George got up unwillingly. Timmy followed her, sniffing expectantly. Soon the two girls were busy getting a fine meal ready, and they all sat on the rocky ledge to eat it.

'Mrs Mackie gave us this enormous bar of chocolate for a present today,' said Anne, showing a great slab to Dick and Nobby. 'Isn't it lovely? No, Pongo, it's not for you. Eat your sandwiches properly, and don't grab.'

'I vote we take some food down into the hill with us,' said Julian. 'We may be quite a long time down there, and we shan't want to come back at tea-time.'

'Oooh – a picnic inside the hill!' said Anne. 'That would be thrilling. I'll soon pack up some food in the kit-bag. I won't bother to make sandwiches. We'll take a new loaf, butter, ham and a cake, and cut what we want. What about something to drink?'

'Oh, we can last out till we get back,' said Julian. 'Just take something to eat to keep us going till we have finished exploring.'

George and Nobby cleared up and rinsed the plates. Anne wrapped up some food in greased paper, and packed it carefully into the kitbag for Julian to carry. She popped the big bar of chocolate into the bag, too. It would be nice to eat at odd moments.

At last they were all ready. Timmy wagged his tail. He knew they were going somewhere.

The five of them pushed the caravan back a few feet to expose the hole. They had all tugged the van back into place the night before, in case Lou and Dan came to go down the hole again. No one could get down it if the caravan was over it.

The boards had been laid roughly across the hole and the boys took them off, tossing them to one side. As soon as Pongo saw the hole he drew back, frightened.

'He's remembered the darkness down there,' said George. 'He doesn't like it. Come on, Pongo. You'll be all right. We've all got torches!'

But nothing would persuade Pongo to go down that hole again. He cried like a baby when Nobby tried to make him.

'It's no good,' said Julian. 'You'll have to stop up here with him.'

'What – and miss all the excitement!' cried Nobby indignantly. 'I jolly well won't. We can tie old Pongo up to a wheel of the van so that he won't wander off. Lou and Dan are away somewhere, and no one else is likely to tackle a big chimp like Pongo. We'll tie him up.'

So Pongo was tied firmly to one of the caravan wheels. 'You stay there like a good chimp till we come back,' said Nobby, putting a pail of water beside him in case he should want a drink. 'We'll be back soon!'

Pongo was sad to see them go – but nothing would have made him go down that hole again! So he sat watching the children disappear one by one. Timmy jumped down, too, and then they were all gone. Gone on another adventure. What would happen now?

Chapter Eighteen

INSIDE THE HILL

THE children had all put on extra jerseys, by Julian's orders, for he knew it would be cold inside the dark hill. Nobby had been lent an old one of Dick's. They were glad of them as soon as they were walking down the dark passage that led to the first cave, for the air was very chilly.

They came to the small cave and Julian flashed his torch to show them where the footholds went up the wall to a hole in the roof.

'It's exciting,' said George, thrilled. 'I like this sort of thing. Where does that hole in the roof lead to, I wonder? I'll go first, Ju.'

'No, you won't,' said Julian firmly. 'I go first. You don't know what might be at the top!'

Up he went, his torch held in his mouth, for he needed both hands to climb. The footholds were strong nails driven into the rock of the cave-wall, and were fairly easy to climb.

He got to the hole in the roof and popped his head through. He gave a cry of astonishment.

'I say! There's a most ENORMOUS cavern here – bigger than six dance-halls – and the walls are all glittering with something – phosphorescence, I should think.'

He scrambled out of the hole and stood on the floor of the immense cave. Its walls twinkled in their queer light, and Julian shut off his torch. There was almost enough phosphorescent light in the cavern to see by!

One by one the others came up and stared in wonder. 'It's like Aladdin's cave!' said Anne. 'Isn't that a queer light shining from the walls – and from the roof, too, Julian?'

Dick and George had rather a difficulty in getting Timmy up to the cavern, but they managed it at last. Timmy put his tail down at once when he saw the curious light gleaming everywhere. But it went up again when George patted him.

'What an enormous place!' said Dick. 'Do you suppose this is where the men hide their stuff, whatever it is?'

Julian flashed his torch on again and swung it round and about, picking out the dark, rocky corners. 'Can't see anything hidden,' he said. 'But we'd better explore the cave properly before we go on.'

So the five children explored every nook and cranny of the gleaming cave, but could find nothing at all. Julian gave a sudden exclamation and picked something up from the floor.

'A cigarette end!' he said. 'That shows that Lou and Dan have been here. Come on, let's see if there's a way out of this great cave.'

Right at the far end, half-way up the gleaming wall, was a large hole, rather like a tunnel. Julian climbed up to it and called to the others. 'This is the way they went. There's a dead match just at the entrance to the tunnel or whatever this is.'

It was a curious tunnel, no higher than their shoulders in some places, and it wound about as it went further into the hill. Julian thought that at one time water must

have run through it. But it was quite dry now. The floor of the tunnel was worn very smooth, as if a stream had hollowed it out through many, many years.

'I hope the stream won't take it into its head to begin running suddenly again!' said George. 'We should get jolly wet!'

The tunnel went on for some way, and Anne was beginning to feel it must go on for ever. Then the wall at one side widened out and made a big rocky shelf. Julian, who was first, flashed his torch into the hollow.

'I say!' he shouted. 'Here's where those fellows keep their stores! There's a whole pile of things here!'

The others crowded up as closely as they could, each of them flashing their torch brightly. On the wide, rocky shelf lay boxes and packages, sacks and cases. The children stared at them. 'What's in them?' said Nobby, full of intense curiosity. 'Let's see!'

He put down his torch and undid a sack. He slid in his hand – and brought it out holding a piece of shining gold plate!

'Coo!' said Nobby. 'So that's what the police were after last year when they came and searched the camp! And it was hidden safely here. Coo, look at all these things. Jumping Jiminy, they must have robbed the Queen herself!'

The sack was full of exquisite pieces of gold plate – cups, dishes, small trays. The childen set them all out on the ledge. How they gleamed in the light of their torches!

'They're thieves in a very big way,' said Julian. 'No doubt about that. Let's look in this box.'

The box was not locked, and the lid opened easily. Inside was a piece of china, a vase so fragile that it looked as if it might break at a breath!

'Well, I don't know anything about china,' said Julian, 'but I suppose this is a very precious piece, worth thousands of pounds. A collector of china would probably give a very large sum for it. What rogues Lou and Dan are!'

'Look here!' suddenly said George, and she pulled leather boxes out of a bag. 'Jewellery!'

She opened the boxes. The children exclaimed in awe. Diamonds flashed brilliantly, rubies glowed, emeralds shone green. Necklaces, bracelets, rings, brooches – the beautiful things gleamed in the light of the five torches.

There was a tiara in one box that seemed to be made only of big diamonds. Anne picked it out of its box gently. Then she put it on her hair.

'I'm a princess! It's my crown!' she said.

'You look lovely,' said Nobby admiringly. 'You look as grand as Delphine the Bareback Rider when she goes into the ring on her horse, with jewels shining all over her!'

Anne put on necklaces and bracelets and sat there on the ledge like a little princess, shining brightly in the magnificent jewels. Then she took them off and put them carefully back into their satin-lined boxes.

'Well – what a haul those two rogues have made!' said Julian, pulling out some gleaming silver plate from another package. 'They must be very fine burglars!'

'*I* know how they work,' said Dick. 'Lou's a wonderful acrobat, isn't he? I bet he does all the climbing about up walls and over roofs and into windows – and Tiger Dan stands below and catches everything he throws down.'

'You're about right,' said Nobby, handling a beautiful silver cup. 'Lou could climb anywhere – up ivy, up pipes – even up the bare wall of a house, I shouldn't wonder! And jump! He can jump like a cat. He and Tiger Dan have been in this business for a long time, I expect. That's where Uncle Dan went at night, of course, when we were on tour, and I woke up and found him gone out of the caravan!'

'And I expect he stores the stolen goods in that wagon of his you showed us,' said Julian, remembering. 'You told us how angry he was with you once when you went and rummaged about in it. He probably stored it there, and then he and Lou came up here each year and hid the stuff underground – waiting till the police had given up the search for the stolen things – and then they come and get it and sell it somewhere safe.'

'A jolly clever plan,' said Dick. 'What a fine chance they've got – wandering about from place to place like that hearing of famous jewels or plate – slipping out at night – and Lou climbing up to bedrooms like a cat. I wonder how they found this place – it's a most wonderful hidey-hole!'

'Yes. Nobody would ever dream of it!' said George.

'And then we go and put our caravan bang on the top of the entrance – just when they want to put something in and take something out!' said Julian. 'I *must* have annoyed them.'

'What are we going to do about it?' said Dick.

'Tell the police, of course,' said Julian, promptly. 'What do you suppose? My word, I'd like to see the face of the policeman who first sees this little haul.'

They put everything back carefully. Julian shone his torch up the tunnel. 'Shall we explore a bit further, or not?' he said. 'It still goes on. Look!'

'Better get back,' said Nobby. 'Now we've found this we'd better do something about it.'

'Oh, let's just see where the tunnel goes to,' said George. 'It won't take a minute!'

'All right,' said Julian, who wanted to go up the tunnel as much as she did. He led the way, his torch shining brightly.

The tunnel came out into another cave, not nearly as big as the one they had left behind. At one end something gleamed like silver, and seemed to move. There was a curious sound there, too.

'What is it?' said Anne, alarmed. They stood and listened.

'Water!' said Julian, suddenly. 'Of course! Can't you hear it flowing along? It's an underground stream, flowing through the hill to find an opening where it can rush out.'

'Like that stream we saw before we came to our caravan camping-place,' said George. 'It rushed out of the hill. Do you remember? This may be the very one!'

'I expect it is!' said Dick. They went over to it and watched it. It rushed along in its own hollowed out channel, close to the side of the cave-wall.

'Maybe at one time it ran across this cave and down the tunnel we came up by,' said Julian. 'Yes, look – there's a big kind of groove in the floor of the cave here – the stream must have run there once. Then for some reason it went a different way.'

'Let's get back,' said Nobby. 'I want to know if Pongo's all right. I don't somehow feel very comfortable about him. And I'm jolly cold, too. Let's go back to the sunshine and have something to eat. I don't want a picnic down here, after all.'

'All right,' said Julian, and they made their way back through the tunnel. They passed the rock shelf on which lay the treasure, and came at last to the enormous gleaming cavern. They went across it to the hole that led down into the small cave. Down they went, Julian and George trying to manage Timmy between them. But it was very awkward, for he was a big dog.

Then along the passage to the entrance-hole. They all felt quite pleased at the idea of going up into the sunshine again.

'Can't see any daylight shining down the hole,' said Julian puzzled. 'It would be near here.'

He came up against a blank wall, and was surprised. Where was the hole? Had they missed their way? Then he flashed his torch above him and saw the hole there – but there was no daylight shining in!

'I say!' said Julian, in horror. 'I say! What do you think's happened?'

'What?' asked everyone, in panic.

'The hole is closed!' said Julian. 'We can't get out! Somebody's been along and put those planks across – and I bet they've put the caravan over them, too. We can't get out!'

Everyone stared up at the closed entrance in dismay. They were prisoners.

'Whatever are we to do?' said George. 'Julian – what *are* we going to do?'

Chapter Nineteen

PRISONERS UNDERGROUND

JULIAN didn't answer. He was angry with himself for not thinking that this might happen! Although Lou and Dan had been seen getting on the bus with bags, they might easily not have been spending the night away – the bags might contain things they wanted to sell – stolen goods of some kind.

'They came back quickly – and came up the hill, I suppose, to have another try at getting Nobby and Pongo back,' said Julian, out loud. 'What an idiot I am to leave things to chance like that. Well – I'll have a try at shifting these planks. I should be able to, with luck.'

He did his best, and did shift them to a certain extent – but, as he feared, the caravan had been run back over the hole, and even if he managed to shift some of the planks it was impossible to make a way out.

'Perhaps Pongo can help,' he said suddenly. He shouted loudly: 'Pongo! Pongo! Come and help!'

Everyone stood still, hoping that they would hear Pongo chattering somewhere near, or scraping at the planks above. But there was no sign or sound of Pongo.

Everyone called, but it was no use. Pongo didn't come. What had happened to him? Poor Nobby felt very worried.

'I wish I knew what has happened,' he kept saying. 'I feel as if something horrid has happened to poor old Pongo. Where can he be?'

Pongo was not very far away. He was lying on his side,

his head bleeding. He was quite unconscious, and could not hear the frantic calls of the children at all. Poor Pongo!

What Julian had feared had actually happened. Lou and Dan had come back up the hill, bringing money with them to tempt Nobby and Pongo back. When they had got near to the hollow, they had stood still and called loudly.

'Nobby! Nobby! We've come to make friends, not to hurt you! We've got money for you. Be a sensible boy and come back to the camp. Mr Gorgio is asking for you.'

When there had been no reply at all, the men had gone nearer. Then they had seen Pongo and had stopped. The chimpanzee could not get at them because he was tied up. He sat there snarling.

'Where have those kids gone?' asked Lou. Then he saw that the caravan had been moved back a little, and he at once guessed.

'They've found the way underground! The interfering little brutes! See, they've moved one of the caravans off the hole. What do we do *now*!'

'This first,' said Tiger Dan, in a brutal voice, and he picked up an enormous stone. He threw it with all his force at poor Pongo, who tried to leap out of the way. But the rope prevented him, and the stone hit him full on the head.

He gave a loud scream and fell down at once, lying quite still.

'You've gone and killed him,' said Lou.

'So much the better!' said Tiger Dan. 'Now let's go and see if the entrance-hole is open. Those kids want their necks wringing!'

They went to the hollow and saw at once that the hole

had been discovered, opened, and that the children must
have gone down it.

'They're down there now,' said Tiger Dan, almost
choking with rage. 'Shall we go down and deal with them
– and get our stuff and clear off? We meant to clear off
tomorrow, anyway. We might as well get the stuff out
now.'

'What – in the daylight – with any of the farm men
about to see us!' said Lou with a sneer. 'Clever, aren't
you?'

'Well, have you got a better idea?' asked Tiger Dan.

'Why not follow our plan?' said Lou. 'Go down when
it's dark and collect the stuff. We can bring our wagon up
as we planned to do tonight. We don't need to bother
about forcing the children to go now – they're underground – and we can make them prisoners till we're
ready to clear off!'

'I see,' said Dan, and he grinned suddenly, showing his
ugly teeth. 'Yes – we'll close up the hole and run the
caravan back over it – and come up tonight in the dark
with the wagon – go down – collect everything – and shut
up the hole again with the children in it. We'll send a
card to Gorgio when we're safe and tell him to go up and
set the kids free.'

'Why bother to do that?' said Lou, in a cruel voice.
'Let 'em starve underground, the interfering little beasts.
Serve 'em right.'

'Can't do that,' said Dan. 'Have the police after us
worse than ever. We'll have to chuck some food down the
hole, to keep them going till they're set free. No good
starving them, Lou. There'd be an awful outcry if we do
anything like that.'

The two men carefully put back the boards over the top of the hole and replaced the heather tufts. Then they ran the caravan back over the place. They looked at Pongo. The chimpanzee was still lying on his side, and the men could see what a nasty wound he had on his head.

'He ain't dead,' said Lou, and gave him a kick. 'He'll come round all right. Better leave him here. He might come to himself if we carried him back to camp, and fight us. He can't do us any harm tonight, tied up like that.'

They went away down the track. Not ten minutes afterwards the children came to the hole and found it blocked up! If only they hadn't stopped to explore that tunnel a bit further, they would have been able to get out and set Timmy on the two men.

But it was too late now. The hole was well and truly closed. No one could get out. No one could find poor Pongo and bathe his head. They were real prisoners.

They didn't like it at all. Anne began to cry, though she tried not to let the others see her. Nobby saw that she was upset, and put his arm round her.

'Don't cry, little Anne,' he said. 'We'll be all right.'

'It's no good staying here,' said Julian, at last. 'We might as well go somewhere more comfortable, and sit down and talk and eat. I'm hungry.'

They all went back down the passage, up through the hole in the roof, and into the enormous cavern. They found a sandy corner and sat down. Julian handed Anne the kitbag and she undid it to get the food inside.

'Better only have one torch going,' said Julian. 'We don't know how long we'll be here. We don't want to be left in the dark!'

Everybody immediately switched off their torches.

The idea of being lost in the dark inside the hill wasn't at all nice! Anne handed out slices of bread and butter, and the children put thin slices of Mrs Mackie's delicious ham on them.

They felt distinctly better when they had all eaten a good meal. 'That was jolly good,' said Dick. 'No, we won't eat that chocolate, Anne. We may want it later on. Golly, I'm thirsty!'

'So am I,' said Nobby. 'My tongue's hanging out like old Timmy's. Let's go and get a drink.'

'Well, there was a stream in that other cave beyond the tunnel, wasn't there?' said Nobby. 'We can drink from that. It'll be all right.'

'Well, I hope it will,' said Julian. 'We were told not to drink water that wasn't boiled while we were caravanning – but we didn't know this sort of thing was going to happen! We'll go through the tunnel and get some water to drink from the stream.'

They made their way through the long, winding tunnel, and passed the shelf of stolen goods. Then on they went and came out into the cave through which the stream rushed so quickly. They dipped in their hands and drank thirstily. The water tasted lovely – so clear and cold.

Timmy drank too. He was puzzled at this adventure, but so long as he was with George he was happy. If his mistress suddenly took it into her head to live underground like a worm, that was all right – so long as Timmy was with her!

'I wonder if this stream *does* go to that hole in the hillside, and pours out there,' said Julian, suddenly. 'If it does, and we could follow it, we might be able to squeeze out.'

'We'd get terribly wet,' said George, 'but that wouldn't matter. Let's see if we can follow the water.'

They went to where the stream disappeared into a tunnel rather like the dry one they had come along. Julian shone his torch into it.

'We could wade along, I think,' he said. 'It is very fast but not very deep. I know – I'll go along it myself and see where it goes, and come back and tell you.'

'No,' said George, at once. 'If you go, we all go. You might get separated from us. That would be awful.'

'All right,' said Julian. 'I thought there was no sense in us all getting wet, that's all. Come on, we'll try now.'

One by one they waded into the stream. The current tugged at their legs, for the water ran very fast. But it was only just above their knees there. They waded along by the light of their torches, wondering where the tunnel would lead to.

Timmy half-waded, half-swam. He didn't like this water-business very much. It seemed silly to him. He pushed ahead of Julian and then a little further down, jumped up to a ledge that ran beside the water.

'Good idea, Tim,' said Julian, and he got up on to it too. He had to crouch down rather as he walked because his head touched the roof of the tunnel if he didn't – but at least his legs were out of the icy-cold water! All the others did the same, and as long as the ledge ran along beside the stream they all walked along it.

But at times it disappeared and then they had to wade in the water again, which now suddenly got deeper. 'Gracious! It's almost to my waist,' said Anne. 'I hope it doesn't get any deeper. I'm holding my clothes up as high as I can, but they'll get soaked soon.'

Fortunately the water got no deeper, but it seemed to go faster. 'We're going down hill a bit,' said Julian at last. 'Perhaps we are getting near to where it pours out of the hill.'

They were! Some distance ahead of him Julian suddenly saw a dim light, and wondered whatever it could be. He soon knew! It was daylight creeping in through the water that poured out of the hole in the hillside – poured out in a torrent into the sunshine.

'We're almost there!' cried Julian. 'Come on.'

With light hearts the children waded along in the water. Now they would soon be out in the warm sunshine. They would find Pongo, and race down the hill in the warmth, catch the first bus, and go to the police station.

But nothing like that happened at all. To their enormous disappointment the water got far too deep to wade through, and Nobby stopped in fright. 'I dursent go no further,' he said. 'I'm almost off my feet now with the water rushing by.'

'I am, too,' said Anne, frightened.

'Perhaps I can swim out,' said Julian, and he struck out. But he gave it up in dismay, for the torrent of water was too much for him, and he was afraid of being hurled against the rocky sides and having his head cracked.

'It's no good,' he said, gloomily. 'No good at all. All that wading for nothing. It's far too dangerous to go any further – and yet daylight is only a few yards ahead. It's too sickening for words.'

'We must go back,' said George. 'I'm afraid Timmy will be drowned if we don't. Oh, dear – we must go all that way back!'

Chapter Twenty

MORE EXCITEMENT

It was a very sad and disappointed little company that made their way back to the cave. Along the tunnel they went, painfully and slowly, for it was not so easy against the current. Julian shivered; he was wet through with trying to swim.

At last they were back in the cave through which the stream flowed so swiftly. 'Let's run round and round it to get warm,' said Julian. 'I'm frozen. Dick, let me have one of your dry jerseys. I must take off these wet ones.'

The children ran round and round the cave, pretending to race one another, trying to get warm. They did get warm in the end, and sank down in a heap on some soft sand in a corner, panting. They sat there for a little while to get their breath.

Then they heard something. Timmy heard it first and growled. 'Jumping Jiminy, what's up with Timmy?' said Nobby, in fright. He was the most easily scared of the children, probably because of the frights he had had the last few days.

They all listened, George with her hand on Timmy's collar. He growled again, softly. The noise they all heard was a loud panting coming from the stream over at the other side of the cave!

'Someone is wading up the stream,' whispered Dick, in astonishment. 'Did they get in at the place where we couldn't get out? They must have!'

'But who is it?' asked Julian. 'Can't be Lou or Dan. They wouldn't come that way when they could come the right way. Sh! Whoever it is, is arriving in the cave. I'll shut off my torch.'

Darkness fell in the cave as the light from Julian's torch was clicked off. They all sat and listened, and poor Nobby shook and shivered. Timmy didn't growl any more, which was surprising. In fact, he even wagged his tail!

There was a sneeze from the other end of the cave – and then soft footsteps padded towards them. Anne felt as if she must scream. WHO was it?

Julian switched on his torch suddenly, and its light fell on a squat, hairy figure, halting in the bright glare. It was Pongo!

'It's *Pongo*!' everyone yelled, and leapt up at once. Timmy ran over to the surprised chimpanzee and sniffed round him in delight. Pongo put his arms round Nobby and Anne.

'Pongo! You've escaped! You must have bitten through your rope!' said Julian. 'How clever you are to find your way through that hole where the stream pours out. How did you know you would find us here! Clever Pongo.'

Then he saw the big wound on poor Pongo's head. 'Oh look!' said Julian. 'He's been hurt! I expect those brutes threw a stone at him. Poor old Pongo.'

'Let's bathe his head,' said Anne. 'I'll use my hanky.'

But Pongo wouldn't let anyone touch his wound, not even Nobby. He didn't snap or snarl at them, but simply held their hands away from him, and refused to leave go. So nobody could bathe his head or bind it up.

'Never mind,' said Nobby at last, 'Animals' wounds often heal up very quickly without any attention at all. He won't let us touch it, that's certain. I expect Lou and Dan hit him with a stone, and knocked him unconscious when they came. They then shut up the hole and made us prisoners. Beasts!'

'I say,' suddenly said Dick. 'I say! I've got an idea. I don't know if it will work – but it really *is* an idea.'

'What?' asked everyone, thrilled.

'Well – what about tying a letter round Pongo's neck and sending him out of the hole again, to take the letter to the camp?' said Dick. 'He won't go to Lou or Dan because he's scared of them – but he'd go to any of the others all right, wouldn't he? Larry would be the best one. He seems to be a good fellow.'

'Would Pongo understand enough to do all that, though?' asked Julian, doubtfully.

'We could try him,' said Nobby. 'I do send him here and there sometimes, just for fun – to take the elephant's bat to Larry, for instance – or to put my coat away in my caravan.'

'Well, we could certainly try,' said Dick. 'I've got a notebook and a pencil. I'll write a note and wrap it up in another sheet, pin it together and tie it round Pongo's neck with a bit of string.'

So he wrote a note. It said:

'To whoever gets this note – please come up the hill to the hollow where there are two caravans. Under the red one is the entrance to an underground passage. We are prisoners inside the hill. Please rescue us soon.

             Julian, Dick, George, Anne and Nobby.'

He read it out to the others. Then he tied the note round Pongo's neck. Pongo was surprised, but fortunately did not try to pull it off.

'Now, you give him his orders,' said Dick to Nobby. So Nobby spoke slowly and importantly to the listening chimpanzee.

'Where's Larry? Go to Larry, Pongo. Fetch Larry. Go. GO!'

Pongo blinked at him and made a funny little noise as if he was saying: 'Please, Nobby, I don't want to go.'

Nobby repeated everything again. 'Understand Pongo? I think you do. GO, then, GO. GO!'

And Pongo turned and went! He disappeared into the stream, splashing along by himself. The children watched him as far as they could by the light of their torches.

'He really is clever,' said Anne. 'He didn't want to go a bit, did he? Oh, I do hope he finds Larry, and that Larry sees the note and reads it and sends someone to rescue us.'

'I hope the note doesn't get all soaked and pulpy in the water,' said Julian, rather gloomily. 'Gosh, I wish I wasn't so cold. Let's run round a bit again, then have a piece of chocolate.'

They ran about and played 'he' for a time till they all felt warm again. Then they decided to sit down and have some chocolate, and play some sort of guessing game to while away the time. Timmy sat close to Julian, and the boy was very glad.

'He's like a big hot-water bottle,' he said. 'Sit closer, Tim. That's right. You'll soon warm me up!'

It was dull after a time, sitting in the light of one torch, for they dared not use them all. Already it seemed as if Julian's torch was getting a little dim. They played all the games they could think of and then yawned.

'What's the time? I suppose it must be getting dark outside now. I feel quite sleepy.'

'It's nine o'clock almost,' said Julian. 'I hope Pongo has got down to the camp all right and found someone. We could expect help quite soon, if so.'

'Well, then, we'd better get along to the passage that leads to the hole,' said Dick, getting up. 'It's quite likely that if Larry or anyone else comes they'll not see the foot-holds leading up the wall out of that first little cave. They might not know where we were!'

This seemed very likely. They all made their way down the tunnel that led past the hidden store of valuables, and came out into the enormous cave. There was a nice sandy corner just by the hole that led down into the first small cave, and the children decided to sit there, rather than in the passage or in the first rocky and uncomfortable little cave. They cuddled up together for warmth, and felt hungry.

Anne and Nobby dozed off to sleep. George almost fell asleep, too. But the boys and Timmy kept awake, and talked in low voices. At least, Timmy didn't talk, but wagged his tail whenever either Dick or Julian said anything. That was his way of joining in their conversation.

After what seemed a long while Timmy growled, and the two boys sat up straight. Whatever it was that Timmy's sharp ears had heard, they had heard nothing at all. And they continued to hear nothing. But Timmy went on growling.

Julian shook the others awake. 'I believe help has come,' he said. 'But we'd better not go and see in case it's

Dan and Lou come back. So wake up and look lively!'

They were all wide awake at once. Was it Larry come in answer to their note – or was it those horrid men, Tiger Dan and Lou the acrobat?

They soon knew! A head suddenly poked out of the hole nearby, and a torch shone on them. Timmy growled ferociously and struggled to fly at the head, but George held on firmly to his collar, thinking it might be Larry.

But it wasn't! It was Lou the acrobat, as the children knew only too well when they heard his voice. Julian shone his torch on to him.

'I hope you've enjoyed your little selves,' came Lou's harsh voice. 'And you keep that dog under control, boy, or I'll shoot him. See? I'm not standing no nonsense from that dog this time. Have a look at this here gun!'

To George's horror she saw that Lou was pointing a gun at poor Timmy. She gave a scream and flung herself in front of him. 'Don't you dare to shoot my dog! I'll – I'll – I'll . . .'

She couldn't think of anything bad enough to do to the man who could shoot Timmy, and she stopped, choked by tears of rage and fear. Timmy, not knowing what the gun was, couldn't for the life of him understand why George wouldn't let him get at his enemy – such a nice position, too, with his head poking through a hole like that. Timmy felt he could deal with that head very quickly.

'Now, you kids, get up and go into that tunnel,' said Lou. 'Go on – go right ahead of me, and don't dare to stop. We've got work to do here tonight, and we're not going to have any more interference from kids like you. See?'

The children saw quite well. They began to walk towards the entrance of the tunnel. One by one they
climbed into it. George first with Timmy. She dared not
let his collar go for an instant. A few paces behind them
came Lou with his revolver, and Dan with a couple of
big sacks.

The children were made to walk right past the shelf on
which were the hidden goods.

Then Lou sat down in the tunnel, his torch switched
on fully so that he could pick out each child. He still
pointed his revolver at Timmy.

'Now we'll get on,' he said to Tiger Dan. 'You know
what to do. Get on with it.'

Tiger Dan began to stuff the things into one of the big
sacks he had brought. He staggered off with it. He came
back in about ten minutes and filled the other sack. It was

plain that the men meant to take everything away this time.

'Thought you'd made a very fine discovery, didn't you?' said Lou, mockingly, to the children. 'Ho, yes – very smart you were! See what happens to little smarties like you – you're prisoners – and here you'll stay for two or three days!'

'What do you mean?' said Julian, in alarm. 'Surely you wouldn't leave us here to starve?'

'Not to starve. We're too fond of you,' grinned Lou. 'We'll chuck you down some food into the tunnel. And in two or three days maybe someone will come and rescue you.'

Julian wished desperately that Pongo would bring help before Lou and Dan finished their business in the tunnel and went, leaving them prisoners. He watched

Tiger Dan, working quickly, packing everything, carrying it off, coming back again, and packing feverishly once more. Lou sat still with his torch and revolver, enjoying the scared faces of the girls and Nobby. Julian and Dick put on a brave show which they were far from feeling.

Tiger Dan staggered away with another sackful. But he hadn't been gone for more than half a minute before a wail echoed through the tunnel.

'Lou! Help! Help! Something's attacking me! HELP.'

Lou rose up and went swiftly down the tunnel. 'It's Pongo, I bet it's old Pongo,' said Julian thrilled.

Chapter Twenty-one

DICK HAS A GREAT IDEA!

'LISTEN,' said Dick, in an urgent voice. 'It may be Pongo by himself – he may not have gone back to the camp at all – he may have wandered about and at last gone down the entrance-hole by the caravans, and come up behind Tiger Dan. If so he won't have much chance because Lou's got a gun and will shoot him. And we shan't be rescued. So I'm going to slip down the tunnel while there's a chance and hide in the big cave.'

'What good will that do?' said Julian.

'Well, idiot, I may be able to slip down into the passage that leads to the entrance hole and hop out without the others seeing me,' said Dick, getting up. 'Then I can fetch help, see? You'd better all clear off somewhere and hide – find a good place, Julian, in case the men come after you when they find one of us is gone. Go on.'

Without another word the boy began to walk down the tunnel, past the rocky shelf on which now very few goods were left, and then came to the enormous cave.

Here there was a great noise going on, for Pongo appeared to have got hold of both men at once! Their torches were out, and Lou did not dare to shoot for fear of hurting Dan. Dick could see very little of this; he could only hear snarlings and shouting. He took a wide course round the heaving heap on the floor and made his way as quickly as he could in the dark to where he thought the hole was that led down into the first passage. He had to go carefully for fear of falling down it. He found it at last and let himself down into the cave below, and then, thinking it safe to switch on his torch in the passage he flashed it in front of him to show him the way.

It wasn't long before he was out of the hole and was speeding round the caravans. Then he stopped. A thought struck him. He could fetch help all right – but the men would be gone by then! They had laid their plans for a getaway with all the goods; there was no doubt about that.

Suppose he put the boards over the hole, ramming them in with all his strength, and then rolled some heavy stones on top? He couldn't move the caravan over the boards, for it was far too heavy for a boy to push. But heavy stones would probably do the trick. The men would imagine that it was the caravan overhead again!

In great excitement Dick put back the boards, lugging them into place, panting and puffing. Then he flashed his torch round for stones. There were several small rocks nearby. He could not lift them, but he managed to roll them to the boards. Plonk! They went on to them one by one. Now nobody could move the boards at all.

'I know I've shut the others in with the men,' thought Dick. 'But I hope Julian will find a very safe hiding-place just for a time. Gosh, I'm hot! Now, down the hill I go – and I hope I don't lose my way in the darkness!'

Down below, the two men had at last freed themselves from the angry chimpanzee. They were badly bitten and mauled, but Pongo was not as strong and savage as usual because of his bad head-wound. The men were able to drive him off at last, and he went limping in the direction of the tunnel, sniffing out the children.

He would certainly have been shot if Lou could have found his revolver quickly enough. But he could not find it in the dark. He felt about for his torch, and found that although it was damaged, he could still put on the light by knocking it once or twice on the ground. He shone it on to Dan.

'We ought to have looked out for that ape when we saw he was gone,' growled Dan. 'He had bitten his rope through. We might have known he was somewhere about. He nearly did for me, leaping on me like that out of the darkness. It was lucky he flung himself on to my sack and not me.'

'Let's get the last of the things and clear out,' said Lou, who was badly shaken up. 'There's only one more load. We'll get back to the tunnel, scare the life out of those kids once more, shoot Pongo if we can, and then clear out. We'll chuck a few tins of food down the hole and then close it up.'

'I'm not going to risk meeting that chimp again,' said Dan. 'We'll leave the rest of the things. Come on. Let's go.'

Lou was not particularly anxious to see Pongo again either. Keeping his torch carefully switched on and his revolver ready, he followed Dan to the hole that led down to the first cave. Down they went, and then along the passage, eager to get out into the night and go with their wagon down the track.

They got a terrible shock when they found that the hole was closed. Lou shone his torch upwards, and gazed in amazement at the underside of the boards. Someone had put them back into place again. *They* were prisoners now!

Tiger Dan went mad. One of his furious rages overtook him, and he hammered against those boards like a
mad-man. But the heavy stones held them down, and the
raging man dropped down beside Lou.

'Can't budge the boards! Someone must have put the
caravan overhead again. We're prisoners!'

'But who's made us prisoners? Who's put back those
boards?' shouted Lou, almost beside himself with fury.
'Could those kids have slipped by us when we were
having that fight with the chimp?'

'We'll go and see if the kids are still there,' said Tiger
Dan, grimly. 'We'll find out. We'll make them very,
very sorry for themselves. Come on.'

The two men went back again to the tunnel. The
children were not there. Julian had taken Dick's advice
and had gone off to try and find a good hiding-place.
He had suddenly thought that perhaps Dick might get
the idea of shutting up the entrance-hole – in which case
the two men would certainly be furious!

So up the tunnel the children went, and into the cave
with the stream. It seemed impossible to find any hiding-
place there at all.

'I don't see where we can hide,' said Julian, feeling
rather desperate. 'It's no good wading down that stream
again – we shall only get wet and cold – and we have no
escape from there at all if the men should come after us!'

'I can hear something,' said George, suddenly. 'Put
your light out, Julian – quick!'

The torch was snapped off, and the children waited in
the darkness. Timmy didn't growl. Instead George felt
that he was wagging his tail.

'It's someone friendly,' she whispered. 'Over there.

Perhaps it's Pongo. Put the torch on again.'

The light flashed out, and picked out the chimpanzee, who was coming towards them across the cave. Nobby gave a cry of joy.

'Here's old Pongo again!' he said. 'Pongo, did you go to the camp? Did you bring help?'

'No – he hasn't been down to the camp,' said Julian, his eyes catching sight of the note still tied round the chimpanzee's neck. 'There's our letter still on him. Blow!'

'He's clever – but not clever enough to understand a difficult errand like that,' said George.

'Oh, Pongo – and we were depending on you! Never mind – perhaps Dick will escape and bring help. Julian, where *shall* we hide?'

'*Up* the stream?' suddenly said Anne. 'We've tried going *down* it. But we haven't tried going up it. Do you think it would be any good?'

'We could see,' said Julian, doubtfully. He didn't like this business of wading through water that might suddenly get deep. 'I'll shine my torch up the stream and see what it looks like.'

He went to the stream and shone his light up the tunnel from which it came. 'It seems as if we might walk along the ledge beside it,' he said. 'But we'd have to bend almost double – and the water runs so fast just here we must be careful not to slip and fall in.'

'I'll go first,' said Nobby. 'You go last, Julian. The girls can go in the middle with Pongo and Timmy.'

He stepped on to the narrow ledge inside the rocky tunnel, just above the rushing water. Then came Pongo. Then Anne, then George and Timmy – and last of all Julian.

But just as Julian was disappearing, the two men came
into the cave, and by chance Lou's torch shone right on
to the vanishing Julian. He gave a yell.

'There's one of them – look, over there! Come on!'

The men ran to where the stream came out of the
tunnel, and Lou shone his torch up it. He saw the line of
children, with Julian last of all. He grabbed hold of the
boy and pulled him back.

Anne yelled when she saw Julian being pulled back.
Nobby had a dreadful shock. Timmy growled ferociously,
and Pongo made a most peculiar noise.

'Now look here,' came Lou's voice, 'I've got a gun,
and I'm going to shoot that dog and that chimp if they
so much as put their noses out of here. So hang on to
them if you want to save their lives!'

He passed Julian to Tiger Dan, who gripped the boy
firmly by the collar. Lou shone his torch up the tunnel
again to count the children. 'Ho, there's Nobby,' he
said. 'You come on out here, Nobby.'

'If I do, the chimp will come out too,' said Nobby.
'You know that. And he may get *you* before you get him!'

Lou thought about that. He was afraid of the big
chimpanzee. 'You stay up there with him, then,' he said.
'And the girl can stay with you, holding the dog. But
the other boy can come out here.'

He thought that George was a boy. George didn't
mind. She liked people to think she was a boy. She
answered at once.

'I can't come. If I do the dog will follow me, and I'm
not going to have him shot.'

'You come on out,' said Lou, threateningly. 'I'm going
to show you two boys what happens to kids who keep

spying and interfering. Nobby knows what happens, don't you, Nobby? He's had his lesson. And you two boys are going to have yours, too.'

Dan called to him. 'There ought to be another girl there, Lou. I thought Nobby said there were two boys and two girls. Where's the other girl?'

'Gone further up the tunnel, I suppose,' said Lou, trying to see. 'Now, you boy – come on out!'

Anne began to cry. 'Don't go, George; don't go. They'll hurt you. Tell them you're a . . .'

'Shut up,' said George, fiercely. She added, in a whisper: 'If I say I'm a girl they'll know Dick is missing, and will be all the angrier. Hang on to Timmy.'

Anne clutched Timmy's collar in her trembling hand. George began to walk back to the cave. But Julian was not going to let George be hurt. She might like to think of herself as a boy, but he wasn't going to let her be treated like one. He began to struggle.

Lou caught hold of George as she came out of the tunnel – and at the same moment Julian managed to kick high in the air, and knocked Lou's torch right out of his hand. It flew up into the roof of the cave and fell somewhere with a crash. It went out. Now the cave was in darkness.

'Get back into the tunnel, George, with Anne,' yelled Julian. 'Timmy, Timmy, come on! Pongo, come here!'

'I don't want Timmy to be shot!' cried out George, in terror, as the dog shot past her into the cave.

Even as she spoke a shot rang out. It was Lou, shooting blindly at where he thought Timmy was. George screamed.

'Oh, Timmy, Timmy! You're not hurt, are you?'

Chapter Twenty-two

THE END OF THE ADVENTURE

No, Timmy wasn't hurt. The bullet zipped past his head and struck the wall of the cave. Timmy went for Lou's legs. Down went the man with a crash and a yell, and the revolver flew out of his hand. Julian heard it slithering across the floor of the cave, and he was very thankful.

'Put on your torch, George, quickly!' he yelled. 'We must see what we're doing. Goodness, here's Pongo now!'

Tiger Dan gave a yell of fright when the torch flashed on and he saw the chimpanzee making straight for him. He dealt the ape a smashing blow on the face that knocked him down, and then turned to run. Lou was trying to keep Timmy off his throat, kicking frantically at the excited dog.

Dan ran to the tunnel – and then stopped in astonishment. Four burly policemen were pushing their way out of the tunnel, led by Dick! One of them carried a revolver in his hand. Dan put his hands up at once.

'Timmy! Come off!' commanded George, seeing that there was now no need for the dog's delighted help. Timmy gave her a reproachful glance that said: 'Mistress! I'm really enjoying myself! Let me eat him all up!'

Then the dog caught sight of the four policemen and yelped furiously. More enemies! He would eat the lot.

'What's all this going on?' said the first man, who was an Inspector. 'Get up, you on the floor. Go on, get up!'

Lou got up with great difficulty. Timmy had nipped

him in various places. His hair was over his eyes, his clothes were torn. He stared at the policemen, his mouth open in the utmost surprise. How had they come here? Then he saw Dick.

'So one of you kids slipped out – and shut the boards on us!' he said, savagely. 'I might have guessed. You . . .'

'Hold your tongue, Lewis Allburg,' rapped out the Inspector. 'You can talk when we tell you. You'll have quite a lot of talking to do, to explain some of the things we've heard about you.'

'Dick! How did you get here so soon?' cried Julian, going over to his brother. 'I didn't expect you for hours! Surely you didn't go all the way to the town and back?'

'No. I shot off to the farm, woke up the Mackies, used their telephone and got the police up here double-quick in their car,' said Dick, grinning. 'Everyone all right? Where's Anne? And Nobby?'

'There they are – just coming out of the tunnel, up-stream,' said Julian, and swung his torch round. Dick saw Anne's white, scared face, and went over to her.

'It's all right,' he said. 'The adventure is over, Anne! You can smile again!'

Anne gave a watery sort of smile. Pongo took her hand and made little affectionate noises, and that made her smile a little more. George called Timmy to her, afraid that he might take a last nip at Lou.

Lou swung round and stared at her. Then he looked at Dick and Julian. Then at Anne.

'So there *was* only one girl!' he said. 'What did you want to tell me there were two boys and two girls for?' he said to Nobby.

'Because there were,' answered Nobby. He pointed to

George. 'She's a girl, though she looks like a boy. And she's as good as a boy any day.'

George felt proud. She stared defiantly at Lou. He was now in the grip of a stout policeman, and Tiger Dan was being hustled off by two more.

'I think we'll leave this rather gloomy place,' said the Inspector, putting away the notebook he had been hastily scribbling in. 'Quick march!'

Julian led the way down the tunnel. He pointed out the shelf where the men had stored their things, and the Inspector collected the few things that were still left. Then on they went, Tiger Dan muttering and growling to himself.

'Will they go to prison?' whispered Anne to Dick.

'You bet,' said Dick. 'That's where they ought to have gone long ago. Their burglaries have been worrying the police for four years!'

Out of the tunnel and into the cave with gleaming walls. Then down the hole and into the small cave and along the narrow passage to the entrance-hole. Stars glittered over the black hole, and the children were very thankful to see them. They were tired of being underground!

Lou and Dan did not have a very comfortable journey along the tunnels and passages, for their guards had a very firm hold of them indeed. Once out in the open they were handcuffed and put into the large police car that stood a little way down the track.

'What are you children going to do?' asked the big Inspector, who was now at the wheel of the car. 'Hadn't you better come down into the town with us after this disturbing adventure?'

'Oh, no thanks,' said Julian politely. 'We're quite used to adventures. We've had plenty, you know. We shall be all right here with Timmy and Pongo.'

'Well, I can't say I'd like a chimpanzee for company myself,' said the Inspector. 'We'll be up here in the morning, looking round and asking a few questions, which I'm sure you'll be pleased to answer. And many thanks for your help in capturing two dangerous thieves!'

'What about the wagon of goods?' asked Dick. 'Are you going to leave it up here? It's got lots of valuables in it.'

'Oh, one of the men is driving down,' said the Inspector, nodding towards a policeman, who stood near by. 'He'll follow us. He can drive a horse all right. Well, look after yourselves. See you tomorrow!'

The car started up suddenly. The Inspector put her into gear, took off the brake and the car slid quietly down the hill, following the winding track. The policeman with the wagon followed slowly, clicking to the horse, which didn't seem at all surprised to have a new driver.

'Well, that's that!' said Julian thankfully. 'I must say we were well out of that. Gosh, Dick, I was glad to see you back with those bobbies so quickly. That was a brain wave of yours to telephone from the farm.'

Dick suddenly yawned. 'It must be frightfully late!' he said. 'Long past the middle of the night. But I'm so fearfully hungry that I simply must have something to eat before I fall into my bunk!'

'Got anything, Anne?' asked Julian.

Anne brightened up at once. 'I'll see,' she said. 'I can find something, I'm sure!'

And she did, of course. She opened two tins of sardines and made sandwiches, and she opened two tins of peaches, so they had a very nice meal in the middle of the night! They ate it sitting on the floor of George's caravan. Pongo had as good a meal as anyone, and Timmy crunched at one of his bones.

It didn't take them long to go to sleep that night. In fact they were all so sleepy when they had finished their meal that nobody undressed! They clambered into the bunks just as they were and fell asleep at once. Nobby curled up with Pongo, and Timmy, as usual, was on George's feet. Peace reigned in the caravans – and tonight no one came to disturb them!

All the children slept very late the next morning. They were awakened by a loud knocking on Julian's caravan. He woke up with a jump and yelled out:

'Yes! Who is it?'

'It's us,' said a familiar voice, and the door opened. Farmer Mackie and his wife peeped in, looking rather anxious.

'We wondered what had happened,' said the farmer. 'You rushed out of the farmhouse when you had used the 'phone last night and didn't come back.'

'I ought to have slipped back and told you,' said Dick, sitting up with his hair over his eyes. He pushed it back. 'But I forgot. The police went down into the hills with us and got the two men. They're well-known burglars. The police got all the goods, too. It was a very thrilling night. Thanks most awfully for letting me use the 'phone.'

'You're very welcome,' said Mrs Mackie. 'And look – I've brought you some food.'

She had two baskets stacked with good things. Dick felt wide awake and very hungry when he saw them. 'Oh, thanks,' he said gratefully. 'You *are* a good sort!'

Nobby and Pongo suddenly uncurled themselves from their pile of rugs, and Mrs Mackie gave a squeal.

'Land-snakes, what's that? A monkey?'

'No, an ape, Mam,' said Nobby politely. 'He won't hurt you. Hi, take your hand out of that basket!'

Pongo, who had been hoping to find a little titbit unnoticed, covered his face with his hairy paw and looked through his fingers at Mrs Mackie.

'Look at that now – he's like a naughty child!' said Mrs Mackie. 'Isn't he, Ted?'

'He is that,' said the farmer. 'Queer sort of bedfellow, I must say!'

'Well, I must be getting along,' said Mrs Mackie, nodding and smiling at George and Anne, who had now come out of their caravan with Timmy to see who the visitors were. 'You come along to the farm if you want anything. We'll be right pleased to see you.'

'Aren't they nice?' said Anne as the two farm-folk went down the cart-track. 'And oh, my goodness – what a breakfast we're going to have! Cold bacon – tomatoes – fresh radishes – curly lettuces – and who wants new honey?'

'Marvellous!' said Julian. 'Come on – let us have it now, before we clean up.'

But Anne made them wash and tidy themselves first! 'You'll enjoy it much more if you're clean,' she said. 'We all look as black as sweeps! I'll give you five minutes – then you can come to a perfectly wonderful breakfast!'

'All right, Ma!' grinned Nobby, and he went off with the others to wash at the spring. Then back they all went to the sunny ledge to feast on the good things kind Mrs Mackie had provided.

Chapter Twenty-three

GOOD-BYE, NOBBY – GOOD-BYE, CARAVANNERS!

BEFORE they had finished their breakfast the Inspector came roaring up the track in his powerful police car. There was one sharp-eyed policeman with him to take down notes.

'Hallo, hallo!' said the Inspector, eyeing the good things set out on the ledge. 'You seem to do yourselves well, I must say!'

'Have some new bread and honey?' said Anne in her best manner. 'Do! There's plenty!'

'Thanks,' said the Inspector, and sat down with the children. The other policeman wandered round the caravans, examining everything. The Inspector munched away at honey and bread, and the children talked to him, telling him all about their extraordinary adventure.

'It must have been a most unpleasant shock for those two fellows when they found that your caravan was immediately over the entrance to the place where they hid their stolen goods.' said the Inspector. 'Most unpleasant.'

'Have you examined the goods?' asked Dick eagerly. 'Are they very valuable?'

'Priceless,' answered the Inspector, taking another bit of bread and dabbing it thickly with honey. 'Quite priceless. Those rogues apparently stole goods they knew to be of great value, hid them here for a year or two till the hue and cry had died down, then got them out and quietly disposed of them to friends in Holland and Belgium.'

'Tiger Dan used to act in circuses in Holland,' said Nobby. 'He often told me about them. He had friends all over Europe – people in the circus line, you know.'

'Yes. It was easy for him to dispose of his goods abroad,' said the Inspector. 'He planned to go across to Holland today, you know – got everything ready with Lou – or, to give him the right name, Lewis Allburg – and was going to sell most of those things. You just saved them in time!'

'What a bit of luck!' said George. 'They almost got away with it. If Dick hadn't managed to slip out when Pongo was attacking them, we'd still have been prisoners down in the hill, and Lou and Dan would have been half-way to Holland!'

'Smart bit of work you children did,' said the Inspector approvingly, and looked longingly at the honey-pot. 'That's fine honey, I must buy some from Mrs Mackie.'

'Have some more,' said Anne, remembering her manners. 'Do. We've got another loaf.'

'Well, I will,' said the Inspector, and took another slice of bread, spreading it with the yellow honey. It looked as if there wouldn't even be enough left for Pongo to lick out! Anne thought it was nice to see a grown-up enjoying bread and honey as much as children did.

'You know, that fellow Lou did some very remarkable burglaries,' said the Inspector. 'Once he got across from the third floor of one house to the third floor of another *across the street* – and nobody knows how!'

'That would be easy for Lou,' said Nobby, suddenly losing his fear of the big Inspector. 'He'd just throw a wire rope across, lasso something with the end of it, top of a gutter-pipe, perhaps, draw tight, and walk across!

He's wonderful on the tight-rope. There ain't nothing he can't do on the tight-rope.'

'Yes – that's probably what he did,' said the Inspector. 'Never thought of that! No, thanks, I really won't have any more honey. That chimpanzee will eat me if I don't leave some for him to lick out!'

Pongo took away the jar, sat himself down behind one of the caravans, and put a large pink tongue into the remains of the honey. When Timmy came running up to see what he had got, Pongo held the jar high above his head and chattered at him.

'Yarra-yarra-yarra-yarra!' he said. Timmy looked rather surprised and went back to George. She was listening with great interest to what the Inspector had to tell them about the underground caves.

'They're very old,' he said. 'The entrance to them used to be some way down the hill, but there was a landslide and it was blocked up. Nobody bothered to unblock it because the caves were not particularly interesting.'

'Oh, but they *are*,' said Anne, 'especially the one with the gleaming walls.'

'Well, I imagine that quite by accident one day Dan and Lou found another way in,' said the Inspector. 'The way you know – a hole going down into the hill. They must have thought what a fine hiding-place it would make for any stolen goods – perfectly safe, perfectly dry, and quite near the camping-place here each year. What could be better?'

'And I suppose they would have gone on burgling for years and hiding the stuff if we hadn't just happened to put our caravan over the very spot!' said Julian. 'What a bit of bad luck for them!'

'And what a bit of good luck for us!' said the Inspector. 'We did suspect those two, you know, and once or twice we raided the circus to try and find the goods – but they must always have got warning of our coming and got them away in time – up here!'

'Have you been down to the camp, mister?' asked Nobby suddenly.

The Inspector nodded. 'Oh, yes. We've been down already this morning – seen everyone and questioned them. We created quite a stir!'

Nobby looked gloomy.

'What's the matter, Nobby?' said Anne.

'I shan't half cop it when I get back to the camp,' said Nobby. 'They'll say it's all my fault the coppers going there. We don't like the bobbies round the camp. I shall get into a whole lot of trouble when I go back. I don't want to go back.'

Nobody said anything. They all wondered what would happen to poor Nobby now his Uncle Dan was in prison.

Then Anne asked him: 'Who will you live with now in the camp, Nobby?'

'Oh, somebody will take me in and work me hard,' said Nobby. 'I wouldn't mind if I could be with the horses – but Rossy won't let me. I know that. If I could be with horses I'd be happy. I love them and they understand me all right.'

'How old are you, Nobby?' asked the Inspector, joining in the talk. 'Oughtn't you to be going to school?'

'Never been in my life, mister,' said Nobby. 'I'm just over fourteen, so I reckon I never will go now!'

He grinned. He didn't look fourteen. He seemed more like twelve by his size. Then he looked solemn again.

'Reckon I won't go down to the camp today,' he said. 'I'll be proper set on by them all – about you going there and snooping round like. And Mr Gorgio, he won't like losing his best clown and best acrobat!'

'You can stay with us as long as you like,' said Julian. 'We'll be here a bit longer, anyway.'

But he was wrong. Just after the Inspector had left, taking his policeman with him, Mrs Mackie came hurrying up to them with a little orange envelope in her hand.

'The telegraph boy's just been up,' she said. 'He was looking for you. He left this telegram for you. I hope it's not bad news.'

Julian tore the envelope open and read the telegram out loud.

'AMAZED TO GET YOUR LETTER ABOUT THE EXTRA-ORDINARY HAPPENINGS YOU DESCRIBE. THEY SOUND DANGEROUS. COME HOME AT ONCE.   DADDY.'

'Oh dear,' said Anne. 'Now we shall have to leave. What a pity!'

'I'd better go down to the town and telephone Daddy and tell him we're all right,' said Julian.

'You can 'phone from my house,' said Mrs Mackie, so Julian thought he would. They talked as they went along and suddenly a bright idea struck Julian.

'I say – I suppose Farmer Mackie doesn't want anyone to help him with his horses, does he?' he asked. 'He wouldn't want a boy who really loves and understands them and would work hard and well?'

'Well, now, I dare say he would,' said Mrs Mackie. 'He's a bit short-handed now. He was saying the other day he could do with a good lad, just leaving school.'

'Oh, *do* you think he'd try our friend Nobby from the

circus camp?' said Julian. 'He's mad on horses. He can do anything with them. And he's been used to working very hard. I'm sure he'd do well.'

Before Julian had left the farmhouse after telephoning to his amazed parents, he had had a long talk with Farmer Mackie – and now he was running back with the good news to the caravans.

'Nobby!' he shouted as he got near. 'Nobby! How would you like to go and work for Farmer Mackie and help with the horses? He says you can start tomorrow if you like – and live at the farm!'

'Jumping Jiminy!' said Nobby, looking startled and disbelieving. 'At the farm? Work with the horses? Coo – I wouldn't half like that. But Farmer Mackie wouldn't have the likes of me.'

'He will. He says he'll try you,' said Julian. 'We've got to start back home tomorrow, and you can be with us till then. You don't need to go back to the camp at all.'

'Well – but what about Growler?' said Nobby. 'I'd have to have him with me. He's my dog. I expect poor old Barker's dead. Would the farmer mind me having a dog?'

'I shouldn't think so,' said Julian. 'Well, you'll have to go down to the camp, I suppose, to collect your few things – and to get Growler. Better go now, Nobby, and then you'll have the rest of the day with us.'

Nobby went off, his face shining with delight. 'Well, I never!' he kept saying to himself. 'Well, I never did! Dan and Lou gone, so they'll never hurt me again – and me not going to live in the camp any more – and going to have charge of them fine farm horses. Well, I never!'

The children had said good-bye to Pongo because he

had to go back with Nobby to the camp. He belonged to Mr Gorgio, and Nobby could not possibly keep him. Anyway, it was certain that even if he could have kept him, Mrs Mackie wouldn't have let him live at the farm.

Pongo shook hands gravely with each one of them, even with Timmy. He seemed to know it was good-bye. The children were really sorry to see the comical chimpanzee go. He had shared in their adventure with them and seemed much more like a human being than an animal.

When he had gone down the hill a little way he ran back to Anne. He put his arms round her and gave her a gentle squeeze, as if to say: 'You're all nice, the lot of you, but little Anne's the nicest!'

'Oh, Pongo, you're really a dear!' said Anne, and gave him a tomato. He ran off with it, leaping high for joy.

The children cleared up everything, put the breakfast things away, and cleaned the caravans, ready for starting off the next day. At dinner-time they looked out for Nobby. Surely he should be back soon?

They heard him whistling as he came up the track. He carried a bundle on his back. Round his feet ran two dogs. Two!

'Why – one of them is Barker!' shouted George in delight. 'He must have got better! How simply marvellous!'

Nobby came up, grinning. They all crowded round him, asking about Barker.

'Yes, it's fine, isn't it?' said Nobby, putting down his bundle of belongings. 'Lucilla dosed him all right. He almost died – then he started to wriggle a bit, she said, and the next she knew he was as lively as could be – bit weak on his legs at first – but he's fine this morning.'

Certainly there didn't seem anything wrong with

Barker. He and Growler sniffed round Timmy, their tails wagging fast. Timmy stood towering above them, but his tail wagged, too, so Barker and Growler knew he was friendly.

'I was lucky,' said Nobby. 'I only spoke to Lucilla and Larry. Mr Gorgio has gone off to answer some questions at the police station, and so have some of the others. So I just told Larry to tell Mr Gorgio I was leaving, and I got my things and hopped it.'

'Well, now we can really enjoy our last day,' said Julian. 'Everybody's happy!'

And they did enjoy that last day. They went down to the lake and bathed. They had a fine farmhouse tea at Mrs Mackie's, by special invitation. They had a picnic supper on the rocky ledge, with the three dogs rolling over and over in play. Nobby felt sad to think he would so soon say good-bye to his 'posh' friends – but he couldn't help feeling proud and pleased to have a fine job of his own on the farm – with the horses he loved so much.

Nobby, Barker, Growler, Farmer Mackie and his wife all stood on the cart-track to wave good-bye to the two caravans the next morning.

'Good-bye!' yelled Nobby. 'Good luck! See you again some time!'

'Good-bye!' shouted the others. 'Give our love to Pongo when you see him.'

'Woof! woof!' barked Timmy, but only Barker and Growler knew what *that* meant. It meant, 'Shake paws with Pongo for me!'

Good-bye, five caravanners ... till your next exciting adventure!

A complete list of the FAMOUS FIVE
ADVENTURES *by Enid Blyton*

Do YOU belong to the FAMOUS FIVE CLUB?

Have YOU got the FAMOUS FIVE BADGE?

There are friends of the FAMOUS FIVE all over the world.

Wear the FAMOUS FIVE badge and you will know each other at once.

If you would like to join the club, send a 20p postal order or postage stamps, but no coins please, with a stamped envelope addressed to yourself, inside an envelope addressed to:

FAMOUS FIVE CLUB
c/o Darrell Waters Ltd
International House
1, St. Katharine's Way
London
E1 9UN

You shall have your badge and a membership card as soon as possible, and your gifts will be used to help and comfort children in hospital.

Jean Webster

DADDY-LONG-LEGS

The story of Judy and her mysterious guardian
is one of the most popular romances ever
written, and it has been both filmed and made
into a highly successful musical.

Judy, at seventeen is taken from an Institution,
where she is the oldest orphan, and sent to
college – at the expense of an amused and
anonymous Trustee. A wavering, elongated
shadow, once seen, is her only clue, and this
induces her to call him Daddy-Long-Legs.

Captain W. E. Johns has, during the past sixty years, written over eighty books about Biggles, the intrepid airman whose adventures take him and his comrades all over the world.

BIGGLES AND THE DARK INTRUDER
BIGGLES BREAKS THE SILENCE
BIGGLES MAKES ENDS MEET
BIGGLES SEES TOO MUCH
BIGGLES FORMS A SYNDICATE
BIGGLES WORKS IT OUT
BIGGLES ON MYSTERY ISLAND